I0645154

THE THREE ISLANDS OF

SUMWHR

ARTHUR H. BARNES

PUBLISHED BY FIDELI PUBLISHING, INC.

Copyright © 2016, Arthur H. Barnes

All Rights Reserved.

No part of this book may be reproduced, stored in a
retrieval system, or transmitted by any means,
electronic, mechanical, photocopying, recording,
or otherwise, without written permission
from the author.

ISBN: 978-1-60414-925-8

Whatever my success at writing, if any, I begin by saying I owe it all to my wife, ALVENA. She and I have been a couple for 64 years and planning many more.

So, thank you, dear lady, you have been my heart, always.

Chapter 1

Josh Roberts tossed a computer printout that contained all the information on Sherwood Investing into the trashcan next to his desk, he leaned back in his simple office chair and wondered, *Is this all there is to life — money, making it, accumulating it, investing it, saving it, spending it?* The last page of the document he'd been reading had said it all. He was a billionaire. All of that material wealth, but for the past few years he'd found no real pleasure in his success.

He turned his chair around so that his view was of the city park. *That's where I want to be, out there in nature with other people, not here reading spreadsheets and counting my wealth. My life has to change soon, or I'm going to lose it.*

He'd traveled to most well known exotic places in the past few years trying to get away from all things he wanted less of in his life, but all those irritations had always found a way back to him regardless of how far he traveled. He didn't want to be a hermit, he was just tired of all the hangers-on, uninteresting people who wanted him in their circles and the relentless groups just waiting for a handout.

The computer screen behind him displayed his wealth in numbers. He knew he couldn't begin to spend all of it, even though he gave generously to many charities. He even donated to various political causes and colleges. He gave all these groups funds, but none of them truly inspired him.

I'd like to find a group or a cause that asks for little and gives much. A group with a cause I could get behind and support whole-heartedly. I just can't find seem to find it.

"Enough of that," he said to himself as he shut down his computer and left his office. He set the security alarm on his way out the door and decided to take a walk through the park before heading home.

On his way to the park, he stopped at a Starbuck's and grabbed a coffee. As he sipped the brew, he took in the parade of humanity passing him by. Eventually, he joined the crowd and headed to the park for a leisurely stroll before dinner.

As the day moved toward evening, he headed to a worn-down part of downtown and his favorite hole-in-the-wall restaurant. He liked to eat there when he had serious thinking to do.

The restaurant in question was located on a side street that gave him a good view when was seated at the only window in the place. He was well known here, and soon became lost in a conversation with the owner, who was also the cook and the waiter.

While he waited for his meal, he took out a small note pad he always carried, and began to make a list of what he thought he wanted to do with the rest of his life. *If I'm going to try to do something worthwhile without being hounded by the media and everyone else, I'll have to look for something outside the U.S.*

Sipping the scotch and soda the owner had set down in front of him, continued to think about items to add to his list. He hadn't made much progress by the time his dinner was set down in front of him. He'd ordered one of his favorites — homemade Italian sausage. Slowly he began to eat, and with each bite, his dilemma continued to nag at him.

He finished his meal and started walking back to his home wondering, *How can I use my talent and money to really do some good? I don't want to just throw money at a problem; I want it to be used on something that really matters.*

Without realizing it, he'd walked back to his office and was standing at the front door when the security guard opened it and asked if he'd forgotten his keys. "No, Bob. I'm fine. I've changed my mind. I think I'll go home. Sorry to bother you."

Chapter 2

For the next month, he took special journeys throughout the city, visiting both the good sections and the bad. His travels didn't make him feel good about the state of things and renewed his feeling that he needed to do something.

Six months later, he was still looking for the answer to exactly what he needed to do to with his life. Even watching the news didn't give him a hint; it just made him more depressed at the state of the world.

One news story detailing the UN's efforts in third world countries caught his attention. *Maybe there is something I can do in one of these countries.* Duly motivated, he requested a special security pass so he could visit some of these countries to see if one of these locations was where his destiny lay.

The result of his request was a pile of forms delivered to him by messenger. He filled out all the information, but as he sealed the envelope something told him this would be just another dead end. *What the heck? I'm going to do this whether I think it's the answer or not. I have to take a chance and start actively doing something or I'm never going to achieve anything,* he thought.

While he waited for his paperwork to clear, he studied the UN and it's members. What he saw was that many of the representatives were corrupt and were only at the UN to line their pockets and escape their pitiful countries. There were a few exceptions, though — most of them from small Asian countries.

Josh knew he wanted to help in a real way, not just throw cash at a problem. *I want to educate people and help them to help themselves,* he thought. *I don't think the UN is the way to go with this. There are just too many countries looking for a sugar daddy rather than an actual long-term solution to their problems.*

Josh was beginning to think that what he was searching for might be out of reach, but he wasn't willing to give up. Maybe his friend Darin at the US Department of Commerce could help. Josh would tell him he was doing research and then pick his brain for some ideas.

Josh had gone to high school with Darin Spence and even though they'd gone to different colleges they'd kept in close touch over the years. Josh wasted no time and called Darin immediately. They agreed to have lunch and discuss what Josh had in mind.

The next day, Josh flew to Washington, DC and checked into the hotel Darin had recommended. Later that evening, they met at a nice restaurant. Before Josh had a chance to even say hello, Darin, asked, "What's your latest million dollar idea?" This was not what Josh expected.

"It's not for profit this time," Josh told him. "I'm looking for a country where the people would benefit from my experience. I want to make a lasting difference. The thing is, I can't seem to find the right location. So far, all I've found is a bunch of politicians with their hands held out for a donation."

"Well, that is a tough thing to figure out," Darin said. "There are a lot of leaders out there who want everything handed to them with no effort on their part. Let me think about this for a while, then tomorrow you can come in to the office and we'll get down to business."

"Sounds good. In return for your help, dinner's on me!"

They spent the remainder of the evening reminiscing and enjoying each other's company.

The next afternoon at Darin's office, Josh was given a short list of potential countries. "I know the list is really short," Darin said, "but your criteria eliminated most of the usual suspects." There were only seven names and none were European countries. Only one African country was listed, though Darin had marked it with a big question mark. Knowing Darin, Josh was sure that this meant he'd be wasting his time there. The other six countries were all in the South Pacific area and the Asian Pacific Rim.

Three on the list were in Malaysia and the other three were islands of the Central Pacific. Now Josh had something to work with and he was ready to tour the locations.

There was nothing to keep him tied to his business so the first item on his list was to divest as many of his holdings and investments as he could to facilitate making his dream a reality once he'd settled on a location. He would need a considerable amount of ready cash, so this first step was an important one.

His next assignment was to exhaustively research each of the locations to learn as much about the culture, governments and needs of each. For several weeks, he plowed through mountains of information. What he learned about most of the locations was discouraging and many were disqualified without a visit.

He continued with his research, remembering his own struggle to create a comfortable place in life and financial stability. There were hard times during that learning process, but it was a valuable experience. Once he got serious about being successful, he'd looked at the way most successful people had gained their wealth. After that, he studied the market from every aspect that he could. After doing some basic math, he had filtered out the so-called losers and invested in those that showed the most promise. He decided to approach his search in much the same way.

Chapter 3

inally, after due diligence, Josh felt it was finally time to visit some of the locations on the list. Almost a year had passed, after all, and he was anxious to get things moving. He took out one of the many travel brochures that cluttered his worktable. "I have to begin somewhere, why not here?" Bali was the locale on the pamphlet he picked up. It was small as far as islands go, but he was familiar with it. He'd spent several pleasant vacations there and now lingered in the memories of those visits.

He slowly picked up the phone and hit the speed dial for his travel agent. A friendly voice answered, "Far out Travel, what can I do to help you?"

"Hi, Lorie—"

As soon as she spoke, the travel agent recognized him and cut in, "Oh it's you, Josh. Where do you want to go this time?"

"Lorie, this time around I want to hit several different locations. I want an open reservation for all but the first destination on my list — Kalsubai, on the Arabian Sea. I'm going on a fact-finding adventure. All of my paperwork is in order, and I'll email you the list of locations. How soon can you set it up for me?"

"Give me about two hours. Do you want me to go ahead and reserve the tickets? You sound like you're in a hurry."

"Sure, go ahead," he said, and hung up.

Shifting as far back in his office chair as he could get, he said, "Okay, I've finally made a commitment, so I'd better get off my tail and start phoning some of the people I want to see. Guess I'd better check out hotels and other accommodations, too. I'll need a place to stay at each location."

Josh gave himself a week to get everything ready. His friend in Kalsubai all but screamed when Josh called and announced his intended visit. "You will, of course, stay with me," he'd said. "No arguments. I have a lot to share with you. Let me know when you will get here and I will meet you at the airport. We have a lot to talk about."

After checking the weather report on his computer, Josh quickly packed for the trip. *I don't think I'll keep a schedule at any point during this trip. I just want to learn about the culture and people of the places I'm going to visit,* he thought as he finished his task.

The trip the next day was grueling. Even though Josh was a frequent traveler, the thirteen hours of steady droning from the plane's engines was giving him a slight headache this time. He was more than a little relieved when the plane finally landed.

His friend met him as he deplaned and hugged him soundly. "I made no definite plans for your stay, since you were so vague when we talked. I am most interested by what you've told me so far, though. How long do you plan to stay?"

"Rega, it's good to see you, my friend. I've made no definite plans for my entire trip. I'll decide what to do based on what I learn from you and others I plan to speak to. How about we find something to eat? The food on the plane was terrible!"

They walked to Rega's older Fiat. The car looked like it had seen too many bumps and grinds — the fender was dented, and the windshield was cracked all the way across.

"Gosh Rega, I thought that you were doing better than this rattletrap indicates. Times must not be so great for you."

Rega just smiled and let Josh know that it did not pay to have a newer car in his country. "You'll see that most of the cars here look the same as mine; they all have battle damage of some sort. The drivers here seem to take an exception undamaged vehicle and try to remedy that as quickly as possible. So, I drive rattletrap and avoid angry drivers. The engine is in very good condition and it serves its purpose. So, what are you doing here, my friend?"

Josh had no response at the moment, since he hadn't fully decided that himself. He wanted to invest in some small country that would make the most of his involvement. "Rega, let's eat and catch up before we get down to business."

Rega took Josh to a small, dingy restaurant. He guaranteed the place served the best Lamb and fish dishes in the country.

Located down a narrow ally, on the second floor, the establishment wasn't what Josh was used to when thinking of a restaurant. It was whitewashed and clean, though, and the man and his daughter who ran the place were friendly.

Rega introduced the man as his cousin, Konsa. The daughter was on the shy side and stayed in the back as Rega gave Josh a little family history.

Finally Rega held out his hand and pulled the daughter and said, "And this is one of the loveliest ladies in all of India. She works here part time while she attends university in town. She plans to become a great surgeon some day. Josh, may I present Simarjit? You'd better be careful. This one will steal your heart."

Josh looked at Simarjit and thought, *She certainly could steal my heart.*

The awkward moment between the two was broken when Konsa asked them to be seated. There were seven small tables in the main dining area and he directed them to on in the back. "We have fresh chicken, some tender young lamb and a rarity in India, tenderloin of beef. What would you like to try?"

Before Josh and Rega could answer, Simarjit let them know that the curry lamb was her father's signature dish. After hearing that, the two decided lamb was their best bet. When their food came, Josh saw the lamb was served on a bed of spicy rice with small vegetables. *Simarit was right; this dish is perfection.*

As they enjoyed the food, Josh began to tell Rega about his new mission in life. "My frustration is that all I've found in my investigations so far is political unrest, corruption in the governments, and a general lack of motivation on the part of the people, probably because of all the corruption. I want to guarantee any money I contribute goes directly to the people, not into the politician's pockets. I think maybe this is going to be difficult to achieve."

"Unfortunately, my friend, that is the way things are done in most of the world. I like what your plan, but it will probably prove to be nearly impossible to achieve your goals here in India. Very few countries, especially on the Asian continent, will let you do anything without dealing with some corrupt officials. It is the only way to get anything done in most places. Maybe you should just give up on this dream and take a long vacation. I'm not sure your ideal location actually exists."

Josh leaned back in his chair. This wasn't what he wanted to hear. He'd been sure there was a section of India where he could realize his dream. After talking to

Rega, though, he was sure he wouldn't find what he was looking for here.

Rega dropped Josh off at his hotel several hours later. Josh was feeling depressed and wondered if what he'd planned would prove impossible to achieve. *Well, I'm not ready to give up yet,* he thought. *I guess the next step is to figure out where I go from here.*

Chapter 4

The first two locations he reviewed brought back fond memories of Bangkok and Thailand and the priceless times that he'd had in Bali. Bali was an especially good memory; because he'd met one of the most beautiful ladies he'd ever seen walking along the beach off of Sanur. She was a local, from one of the modest but influential families of the area. They'd spent time together viewing sunsets over the Java Sea. *I wonder if she's married now,* he mused. *She's probably got a bunch of kids too.*

Josh spent several more days there at Rega's urging. Simarjit helped fill in some of his more pleasant moments, as well.

Rega had done his best to find answers to Josh's questions. Finally, he sat down with Josh and let him know that he'd exhausted his contacts but didn't have good news. All of the countries and politicians wanted to take Josh's money but none would make promises about what they'd do with it. This discouraging news meant

Josh would end his stay in India the following day to go in search of his ultimate beneficiary. He told Rega he would be in touch.

His next stop was Thailand. Josh's stay there was short; no one wanted to talk to him unless he had some kind of plan for improving their economy or standard of living.

While he was there, he stayed in the Royal Orchid Sheraton Hotel in a room overlooking the Chao Phya River — the fabled river of kings. He visited the traditional tourist sites, but nothing really caught his interest. A guide he met on one of the tours offered to give him a more intimate look at the country. Punsak Catysomay, the guide, took Josh on a jungle boat ride out in the wilderness to visit a floating market. "I am sure that you will find the market much more interesting than just walking around Bangkok." This jaunt turned out to be the most interesting thing he saw in Thailand.

Chapter 5

When he'd had his fill of Thailand, Josh decided that Bali had to be a friendlier place to visit. He took the first flight out to Jakarta with a connecting flight to Bali. This stop was more for pleasure than business. He got a nice room at the Hyatt, just off the beach. *This looks like a great place to get some thinking done,* he thought.

After a slow dinner, he decided to take a walk around the hotel. It was huge and new! The grand gardens filled with tropical vegetation brought back fond memories of his time in Thailand. Giant Papaya shrubs full of ripening fruit were growing everywhere.

Fahra, the lobby attendant at the hotel had taken a fancy to Josh. Each time Josh went to the lobby, he would run after him asking if Josh needed anything. A month into Josh's stay, Fahra cornered him and asked, "Why are you spending so much money with the hotel when all you do is sleep in the room?"

"Why would you ask me that, Fahra? Don't you want your employer to make money from my stay?"

"I'm just concerned for you. There are several fine private apartments and small homes that rent for just a few dollars a month. You could have all the privacy you need. You can even have a lady stay with you and a housekeeper. Pretty nice living if you ask me."

Josh hadn't thought about how long he'd stay in Bali and the idea of a private place sounded pretty good. "That sounds like a good idea. Would you happen to know how I'd go about finding such a place?"

"Yes," Fahra replied, "you should go through an agency. The best one is just up the street. My sister works there and she'll make sure they take good care of you."

Josh smiled and added, "I bet she slips you a commission for your efforts."

"Mr. Josh, it is the way of the world. Yes she gives me a small amount for each month someone I recommend stays in a rental. Does that offend you?"

"No, you're right, it is the way of the world."

Josh visited Fahra's sister and she quickly found a suitable rental for him. The pleasant apartment overlooked a deep canyon that had been terraced and cultivated. The rice growing there looked healthy. There were also random banana and cocoanut trees mingled with the rice. The long and wide banana tree leaves seemed to stay in season forever, gently moving back and forth with the almost constant breeze.

Nearly every day, Josh strolled down to the waterfront and watched the small fishing boats come in, sell their day's catch on the dock and then go back out again. After some weeks, he struck up a conversation with one of the boat owners. He and asked him what he did with the bunch of different pots and pans he took with him when he went out to sea for a week at a time. The boatman just ignored Josh and his questions, so the mystery remained.

Chapter 6

On a Saturday afternoon, Josh came upon the same boat owner cleaning his boat. Without any invitation, Josh stepped over the railing and asked if he could help. The man was surprised and told Josh that no one had ever offered to help him. "I would be most honored to have your presence on my old boat. There is no need for you to get yourself wet by washing the deck, though. That is all I have left to do. Please make yourself comfortable on that bench over there until I am finished.

Josh took a seat watched as the man finished his chore. As he sat there, he decided he would make an offer on the man's boat. It made no sense, because he'd never done any fishing or boating, but it seemed like the thing to do.

"What's your name, sir?"

"I go by the name of Grando, don't ask me why. My family called me grande the day I was born," he explained, "but they did not want my name to sound big so they replaced the 'e' with an 'o'. So, Grando I've been for the past forty-some years."

"Well, Grando, I'm enjoying Bali but I need to find something to occupy my mind and keep my brain from turning to Jell-O. I'd like to help you with your business and travel to wherever you go. That way I will be busy doing something. Where do you go when you leave for days?"

Grando quickly replied, "For a number of years, I have traveled to the remote islands around here. I take a supply of household good the islanders need but can't manufacture on their own. It's nothing big, unless someone places a specific order. Mostly I sell pots and good quality pans, specialty knives, tea. They drink a lot of the stuff and it's the only item they consume that's difficult for them to get. I sometimes stop to fish as I go, too. I have a freezer hold down below so I can keep the catch pretty fresh for quite a few days. This adds a nice extra income, especially when I catch a big fisheye tuna. The people in Bali a premium for tuna, so it's worth it."

Josh knew very little about boats and even less about how they worked, so he asked Grando if he would show him the ropes, so to speak. Grando was proud of his vessel and started at the bow, instantly becoming the teacher and telling Josh that the front of every boat or ship is called the bow. He described the anchor and the winch that controlled it, then moved to the stern, and repeated his lessons on what each part of the boat was called.

Next they went below decks. Waiting to brag about the most important part of the boat, Grando began with the fuel storage tanks and then moved on to the cabin. Josh could plainly see that there were two narrow bunks for sleeping. They looked pretty uncomfortable. Grando must have noticed Josh's expression and told him that there was little time for sleeping. "If the boat is underway, I have to be on deck at all times. I wouldn't want to run up on a rock, or worse yet, the beach. There has to be constant safety at all times."

Their final destination was the small live fish tank amidships of the aft part of the deck. This seemed to be the part of the boat Grando was most proud of.

After his tour and lesson, Josh came to an agreement with his new friend, Grando the ocean traveler. Josh would buy all the fuel and pay for any repairs that might be needed. Grando was delighted that he would have a friend to share his days at sea.

Chapter 7

Their first extended journey was to a small group of islands about one hundred miles from Bali. Grando said the trip would take about two weeks if the weather was friendly and gave Josh a serious smile, adding, "We're three hundred miles south of the equator and the weather can change in just a few minutes. Normally, the southern trade winds just refresh the day, but they can turn mean in an instant."

The trip was nothing but beautiful, with blue skies and high-cirrus clouds constantly charging by. The sunsets were far more spectacular than any Josh had ever seen. He'd brought a digital Nikon camera with him and managed to take some great photos along the way. This was the first time he'd ever documented any of his travels and he thought it would be fun to share this experience with his friends back home. For the first time in his life, Josh felt totally content with his life.

Grando's old, wooden-hulled boat had seen far too many miles at sea. The old engine made a sputtering noise when it started, then it would roar and cough out a cloud of dark smoke. Upon returning to Bali, Josh made a big decision. It was time to get a new vessel.

There were no state-of-the-art boat builders in Bali; the best were in Japan and South Korea. Giving Grando a lame excuse about having to check on some of his investments, Josh flew to Japan to see what kind of fortune he would have to pay for a fast, metal-hulled diesel boat. He had no idea what size would be best, so he set about educating himself before vising the builder.

One of the first questions that he asked of a portside fishing boat owner in Kyoto was, "You have a fine metal boat. Can you tell me who makes the best boats like yours?"

"If you have the money," the man replied, "you need to go to Kyoto and talk to Hjosan. He knows everyone and can help you arrange what you need. He won't take advantage of you either. Tell him that Leba sent you. Do you plan to get into fishing?"

"Possibly," Josh replied.

"Well, good luck to you."

Josh thanked him and left for the train station that would take him to Kyoto. He'd had traveled to Kyoto several times in the past and had always found it to be a friendly place.

The train ride south was enjoyable and he enjoyed the lush scenery. He saw several farmers using water buffalo to turn the soil. He was pleased to learn there were still a few traditionalists out there.

When he got to Kyoto, he decided the first order of the day would be finding something to eat. He started walking and eventually saw an older lady standing in front of him stirring something that might be soup. Josh gave her the traditional greeting of "Ohayo" or good morning in Japanese.

She quickly responded, "Gozaimasu, and I do speak some English."

After Josh told her what he was looking for, she invited him to join her in her near-noon tea.

As they talked, Josh mentioned Hjosan's name. Upon hearing this, she smiled and said everyone in Kyoto knew Hjosan. "Hjosan lives on the other side of our beautiful city," Mr. American. "You will have to take a cab if you don't want to walk for hours."

Josh was surprised at being called an American and asked the lady how she knew. "That's easy, Mr. American. It was your accent. We have a flood of Americans visiting our city and it's easy to hear the difference in the way you speak. I'm sure that you will meet many fellow Americans as you go about your business."

When they'd finished their tea, Josh took the woman's advice and got a taxi. He asked the driver to take him to Mr. Hjosan's home, and the driver laughed and said, "Mr. Hjosan lives in his place of business and his business is well known. How did you learn his name?" Josh quickly explained.

The drive seemed to wind through most of the city. Josh was sure that the driver wanted to show him as much of Kyoto as he could. After a while, the taxi came to a stop in front of what looked like an expensive hotel and restaurant.

"Hjosan lives in the top apartment of the building," the taxi driver said. "It is rumored to be one of the finest apartments in all Japan. He is a most generous person and gives much to the city and the poor, not that we have many poor living in Kyoto."

Josh tipped the driver generously and headed into the building. When he asked for Hjosan, a casually dressed gentleman softly spoke and said that he was Hjosan and had been expecting him.

"How did you know I was coming to see you?" Josh asked.

"The lady you had lunch with called me immediately after you got into taxi and let me know you were on your way."

"It seems like everyone in Kyoto knows you," Josh said.

Hjosan ignored the compliment and asked, "Do you have hotel reservations?" Josh hadn't thought that far ahead but was sure suitable accommodations would be easy to find in such a large city.

He told Hjosan as much, and he said, "I have just the place for you. I will give you the address later. Please, let's sit and you can tell me why you've come to see me."

"First, what should I call you? Mr. Hjosan, Hjosan or something else? For some reason, I feel like I've met you before. Possibly a long time ago," Josh said.

"My friend, and I intend to be just that — your trusted friend — and I do have, a first name. It's Kajiro, but I prefer to be addressed as Hjosan. Now, tell me why you're here."

Josh quickly explained what his mission was and stressed that he didn't have any idea how a good boat was built. "I made a list of what the boat captain told me he would some day like to have. He makes trips to the Indonesian Island territory and trades with the people there. He also fishes for big-eyed tuna when he has a chance. I would like your advice on which metal ship builders in the area I should visit. I've heard the builders here are the best."

"There are a number of boat builders that can build one of the safest metal boats in the world. Several of them are my close friends. I will give you their information.

"Now, to the issue of your accommodations. I have a number of extra secure apartments for guests like you. I think you'll find one of them will work for you. Also, I assure you the food you'll get here is better any restaurant. I would consider it my personal privilege to host you in the room of your choice. Come let me show you."

Josh was surprised to see there was a special elevator for the top six floors. Hjosan explained that each visitor got his own key and only that key would allow the elevator to go to his specific floor. The elevator stopped at the top floor and walked down the hall to the room Hjosan had in mind.

They stopped at the very last door and Hjosan said, "My apartment is one door down, so as you can see, we will be neighbors. I hope we can share some interesting conversations and meals. Speaking of food, will you be my guest for dinner? How about six this evening?"

Hjosan exhibited nothing but great pride as he ushered Josh around the apartment. It was far more than Josh could ever have hoped for and he told Hjosan he was overwhelmed and grateful. Before Josh could say anything further, one of Hjosan's men arrived with Josh's belongings and asked, "Would you like me to unpack your suitcase?"

At this point, Hjosan excused himself and said he would look forward to seeing Josh in the dinning room at six. "We can discuss things in further detail then," he said and left Josh to unpack and freshen up.

Chapter 8

Dinner with Hjosan was a constant conversation the travels both had experienced. After dinner, over Saki, Hjosan said, "Okay, my new friend, what do you need from me?"

Josh had drawn what he thought would be the best design for Grando's boat. What he needed help with was how to outfit it. He knew that there had to be much better bunk arrangements, a nicer toilet configuration and galley than what existed on the current boat. He also wanted a freezer area to store fish.

Hjosan took the drawing and smiled. "Friend, I don't know much more than you about boats. In fact, all I really know what true boatmen have told me over the years, 'a boat can be put on a ship but a ship cannot be put on a boat.' I strongly suggest we meet with one of the boat manufactures and let them design your boat. They'll probably make several different drawings and then you can choose what you want. I've called the builder I think can do the best job for you. We can see them tomorrow morning, if you like."

Early the next morning Hjosan found Josh quietly savoring his breakfast in the dining room. Josh was the only person there and was enjoying the quiet time thinking about how he was going to present a challenge for the boat builder.

Hjosan asked, "May I join you? What you're having looks good. I think I'll have the same."

Hjosan told Josh they had an appointment at eight to see the boat builder. "We need to be on time; he's an extremely exact person and values his time."

The boat yard was on the waterfront in a cove. The location offered a spectacular view. Hjosan introduced the boat builder and explained that he'd changed his name to fit his occupation and bring more attention to his craft. "His name is Kobune Tsukuri, or boat builder. He likes to be addressed in that way. He is a very proud craftsman."

The first item on the agenda was the serving of tea. One of the office ladies brought out a steaming pot and asked if they would like to share some of her homemade cakes. "They are a traditional way of greeting friends," she said. "I understand, Mr. Josh, that you are a special friend of our wonderful Hjosan. Welcome."

After they'd finished their tea, Kobune said, "Let's get down to the business of designing your boat, Mr. Josh."

"Please, just call me Josh, just plain Josh."

"Okay, just plain Josh, Hjosan has given me a brief description of what you would like me to build for you. I've heard you have some pencil drawings that might give me an idea of where to start.

After looking at the drawings, Kobune said, "We've built many boats similar to your drawings. Let me show you some photos of a few of our best." Kobune brought out an album and began to flip slowly through it. All of the pages contained photos of fine-looking boats. He expressed the main purpose of each as they viewed them.

As Kobune came to the end of the photos, he said he was sure there were examples that came close to what Josh wanted, they could then customize things until it was exactly what he had in mind. "We only build double-hulled boats. They're much safer."

Kobune went on to explain what a double-hulled boat was and how they were built, including that the inner hull is fabricated from one-quarter inch special aluminum. The outer hull is made of the same material but is five-eights of an inch thick. "That way, if the outer hull is punctured by some foolishness, the inner hull will keep the boat afloat," Kobune concluded.

"Now let's take a walk around the yard so you can see how we do things."

It was dinnertime before Josh, Hjosan and Kobune agreed on what the boat needed to have inside. Kobune suggested that they could begin the basic fabrication the following week. "You and Grando should visit before the upper deck construction begins so you can make sure wheelhouse, the sleeping areas, toilet facilities and galley meet your specifications. We don't want to go forward at that stage without your approval."

Josh and Hjosan were more than pleased with how the day had gone. As they sat sharing one of Hjosan's fine dinners, they went over much of what had happened. Finally, Josh asked if he could spend several days at Hjosan's establishment so he could enjoy being a tourist. He also asked if Hjosan knew of someone who could act as a knowledgeable escort and tell him about the various places he visited.

"How about Omiko? You met her when she served us tea and cakes. She has an advanced degree in Japanese culture and has taught at several universities. I'm sure she is exactly who you're looking for."

As the evening closed, Josh said that he wanted to give Kobune a large advanced draft to start the boat and had no idea what the boat would cost. "We did not discuss the price. I am well prepared to give Mr. Kobune a draft for the total cost of the boat if I knew just how much."

"Josh, one thing you must always remember when dealing with special friends, don't discuss money until absolute satisfaction has been achieved. The time to ask the price is when you come for an inspection of the progress. At this time I don't think he knows what the final price will be. I do know that he will take our friendship into consideration when it comes to figuring the total cost."

Josh considered Hjosan's statement and decided that he had truly found a serious friend he'd have for many years to come. He excused himself, saying he wanted to get a good night's rest before heading off the next day with Hjosan's tour guide. He thanked Hjosan again and went off to bed.

The next day, Josh met Omiko, the tour guide, and she immediately asked, "Do you have a plan or should I begin with some of Japan's history, especially for the area near Kyoto?"

Josh had no idea where what he was interested would be located. "The only place I remember being over-whelmed by is Kamakura, where the giant bronze Buda stands in a beautiful garden. I was so impressed with the story about it being cast in one piece that I wanted to learn more about it and maybe Buddhism too.

"Oniko, why don't you choose the most historical cities and show me where they are on the map. We don't have a schedule, and you can treat it like your vacation if you like but I will pay for your time and all your expenses. Would that be okay with you?

Oniko didn't respond at first, then she softly said, "I think that would be fine. I find you a pleasant and likable person."

"Let's find a teahouse and make a list of some places so we can plan how to get from one place to another. Does that work for you?"

Josh and Omiko spent five delightful days and several evenings visiting all the places they'd listed. When Josh returned to Hjosan's place, he thanked him again for recommending Oniko. "I had a much better time than I thought I would. Now, I need to make reservations so I can fly back to Bali."

Chapter 9

The flight back to Bali was pleasant. Josh spent the time reflecting what Hjosan had shared with him. Warm sunny weather, dark blue skies greeted him when the plane landed. Josh hoped Grando would like the boat he was having built, but was worried that he was a proud person who might be offended by such an expensive gift. *I'll tell him we're sharing it if he has a problem with the idea,* Josh thought. *Plus, I want a better place to sleep than that uncomfortable slab in the old boat.*

Josh couldn't find Grando's boat when he went to the dock. When he asked around, he found out that Grando had moved to a better-arranged harbor and had left the new address and directions so Josh could find him.

When Josh found him, Grando explained the move by saying that he was getting tired of all the junkie old boats and wanted a better pier to tie up to. "Besides, your old apartment wasn't the best place to live. I also thought you needed a place that fits your status.

"I arranged for a new apartment for you. It has a road going directly to Denpasar, the capitol. It's more modern and also near the beach where you can watch the pretty lady tourists."

Before the two men could get to Josh's new apartment, Grando started giving him the schedule for their next adventure. "I haven't been to the beautiful island called Sulawesi in many years. I think you'll enjoy visiting there. You'll see some new faces and learn about a different culture. The island is about 200 miles east of Borneo and maybe the same distance from Bali. It's tropical from one end to the other. The first harbor I think the first port we should visit is called Parepare, on the east side. Then if we want to continue north to Palu, I think that we could add some important markets for the people there. Does that sound okay?"

"Sounds like an adventure to me," Josh said.

"Good, then Sulawesi it is. It'll take me two days to lay in all the supplies and fuel. So, can you be ready at dawn, two days from now?"

The next day, as Grando brought several boxes of supplies onboard the ship, Josh asked if he'd packed several pounds of the best available coffee.

"Coffee? No. Only foreigners drink that bitter stuff. I know the Hyatt serves the best. I'll ask the suppler where I can get some. We'd better decide how long we're going to be gone so I can get enough for the whole trip. I don't think there are very many places where we can get more once we leave here."

Josh didn't think they'd be staying long in any one spot, so he had no idea how much of anything they'd need. "I think maybe twenty pounds should be enough."

One last grunt from Grando let Josh know he would be the only coffee drinker onboard.

The remaining chores went smoothly and they left at dawn on the appointed day. By noon on the third day of their trip they were making good time. Calm seas and warm sunshine made for a pleasant trip, and they were cruising along at about ten knots. "We should be at our first stop by noon tomorrow and maybe have a great dinner if there is such a thing there," Grando said.

"The port is called Pandang. It's on the Southwest side of the main island and has all the best that Sulawesi has to offer. It's not as modern as Bali, but the slow pace and friendly people make it a great place to visit."

"I'm sure we'll enjoy our stay," Josh said; as Grando went on to explain his interest in developing trade with the more important stores there.

They cruised into a busy harbor. Josh hadn't expected so much activity in what he had come to believe was a backwater South Pacific Island. There were lots of small fishing boats and the dock area was crowded. Several boats were even tied together at one station. Why didn't he tell me about the crowds? Josh wondered.

He didn't bother Grando, though since he was busy trying to find a proper place to secure the boat. After a lot of maneuvering, Grando finally muscled his way into an open space next to a much larger boat. He let out a loud grunt of approval that said they were lucky to find such a good place.

The first item on their agenda was finding a good place for dinner. After asking several locals where the best was, they learned that the only good place was a number of streets over toward the center of the town. Both men thought it would be an extra treat to do a little sightseeing on their way. The found the main part of the town was clean and the people were friendly.

They sought out the recommended restaurant and were taken to a table near the front that had an open space where a glass window should've been. There was a gentle offshore breeze coming in the hole, making the close of the day pleasant. They ordered and Josh decided he hadn't had a Scotch as good as the one he was served since he left Japan. Grando preferred cold beer and strong tea, so he ordered one of each.

Their waitress was a young, attractive girl who was wearing a traditional multicolored dress. There was no formal menu; the girl just listed several fish dishes, all of which sounded good. Grando quickly asked, "Is the fish fresh?"

The question seemed to offend the waitress and she responded, "Go catch your own if our fish isn't good enough for you. You look like one of those crazy guys from the fishing docks."

Both men just laughed and said the fish would be fine and was surely the freshest available. This pleased the girl and she asked if they needed another drink to go along with their dinners. Josh and Grando knew they'd found a nice place to spend some of their leisure hours while visiting Pandang.

The next day, the two men toured the city and became acquainted with a number of potential clients that might mean new business for Grando. They also shopped for supplies and restocked the boat for the next leg of their journey. The plan was to travel to Sulawesi's other large port, Kolaka. Grando said he'd visited the port a long time ago but didn't remember much about it.

Somehow, word of their arrival preceded them and several merchants greeted them as they tied up the clean and friendly dock. The merchants were more curious about the two travelers than they were about business.

Grando, always the businessman, explained his reason for the visit and made sure he got several commitments for a later business discussion. Josh enjoyed people watching while Grando conduced business. The local styles were extremely eye-catching. It seemed the men had a long tradition for their style of dress and were most proud of it.

Josh found a busy, but quiet café where he invited several of the men to join him for a drink. He was surprised when all of the men asked for a local brand of beer. There was nothing wrong with the beer, but Josh wasn't sure about it and ordered a more familiar brand.

They spent the afternoon talking and Josh learned a lot from them. As dinnertime arrived, Josh left the men to go find Grando and get some food.

Grando was not to be found. Josh finally asked if anyone had seen a bearded, short man in seaman clothes. That earned a smile and the person asked, "Do you mean that funny little guy wanting to talk the pants off of everyone?"

As Josh was about to give up and eat by himself, Grando came striding along the dirt sidewalk with two men in tow. "Josh, my sailing friend, please meet two of the local businessmen who want to trade some merchandise with me. They're not interested in any long-term plan but gave me a list of items they have a hard time getting here in Sulawesi. How about that?"

"That's great, Grando. Why don't you invite your new friends to dinner? I'm starved." The men agreed and joined Josh in a slow but quality dinner.

They'd been in the port for three days when Josh asked, "How much longer do you plan to stay here?"

"I'm ready to leave when you are my friend," Grando said.

Chapter 10

The next stop they'd planned was the last port on the southeast tip Sulawesi. When they were done there, they'd head back to Bali. They'd traveled some 700 miles, and Josh kept track of everything in his logbook. As promised, Josh paid for all the diesel fuel and oil. He was using this as a way to keep a record of their business venture here. The last port proved uneventful, and they were soon ready to leave.

As they got underway, on their trip back to Bali, Grando poured Josh a fresh cup of coffee and began to explain something that he'd learned while at last port. "Josh, there are three islands we should visit before going back to Bali. They're inhabited people who've lived on the island several thousand years. The person who told me about them said the native people don't really like visitors. In fact, they won't let any foreigner stay overnight.

"He also said they are friendly but cautious. Maybe it's just me being curious, but I think we might learn something useful if we stop there and ask for fresh water and maybe some extra food. Do you want to try?"

"Sounds like a plan."

"The guy didn't know the exact longitude and latitude He said it was somewhere at about 5 degrees south and maybe 125 degrees east. He also said that he'd never visited there himself, but had talked to several people who had."

Josh broke out the area map and plotted the approximate location of the three islands. "Grando, if what you said about the location is even close, it's more miles to our east than it is to go home. Take a heading of south by southeast and let's see if we can find them. I'm feeling a little like the early explorers, you know, Captain Cook or whoever, who found the Hawaiian Islands."

Grando and Josh were surprised by the perfect weather as they sailed south. The sea was like a piece of polished glass and cavorting porpoises played with the bow of their boat. They were traveling at a steady 12 knots, which was the best cruising speed for fuel conservation. It was perfect, and they enjoyed watching the dolphins until they finally left them behind.

On the fourth day, at the close of the evening, an island seemed to materialize out of the sea. It looked like a high mountain with no apparent base. The tip was white, almost like it was covered with snow. Josh wondered if this was actually the case or if it was just a trick of the light. The more he looked, though, the more he was sure that it was a snow-capped mountain.

Finally, Grando cleared things up for him saying he was told there were two mountains on the island and that at times, snow capped tallest one. "I think this means we've found what we've been searching for. We're about thirty miles out and at our present speed, we'll get there after it's dark. That might be a problem, since the guy who told me about this place said the natives aren't too friendly. I think we should wait until daylight tomorrow before we approach, since I have no idea whether there are shoals, rocks or other things that might be rough on the boat."

They anchored about 10 miles from shore and got a good night's sleep.

Early the next morning, they traveled the short distance to the island. Cutting the power to the two diesel engines, Grando slowly crept to the eastern most part of the island, where the highest mountain proudly stood. Just as they were about to drop anchor, a small boat paddled by four men came from out of nowhere and challenged them.

At first the natives were extremely unfriendly, but when they found out the two men only wanted some water, and maybe fresh fruit, their attitudes changes. The men told Josh and Grando they could stay the night and replenish their supplies, including some fresh vegetables.

The mention of fresh vegetables caused both men to look at each other in surprise. Such items were almost unheard of in most of the Pacific area. Grando thanked the men and asked if they'd like to stick around and talk. Grando understood them well enough to get by, but did have to ask them to repeat themselves when he heard strange phrases he didn't recognize.

After a while, they noticed the island men were smiling and enjoying the conversation. With help from Grando, Josh was able to ask them about their culture and history. After their conversation, the islanders decided Josh and Grando were no threat and offered them an anchorage in a more protected bay near the base of the mountain.

Much to Grando and Josh's surprise, the new anchorage had a view of a strange cave-like opening at the mountain's base. The opening was near the small sandy beach where they'd anchored.

When they got settled in their new spot, Grando and Josh just sat staring at each other until they figured out what they wanted to do next. Finally, Josh asked, "Do you want to cook dinner or should I? There's only enough room in the galley for one person at a time."

Grando slowly stood up and said. "If you decide what we're having and get the ingredients together, I'll do the cooking."

After dinner, the two sat on the aft deck and discussed their earlier conversation with the natives. The natural beauty they saw around them also impressed them. There were giant coconut trees, several banana trees with ripening fruit hanging plainly in sight and large papayas with fruit hanging on random bushes. As they talked, Josh realized he needed to know more about the people and the island, and promised Grando he would try to have a long conversation the next day with whoever was in charge.

All night long, Josh tossed and turned. Questions and possibilities flooded his mind and wouldn't let him rest. Near dawn, he finally gave up trying to sleep and got dressed. He was amazed that Grando could sleep so soundly tossing and turning and making so much noise. Grando wasn't bothered and was happily snoring away, completely oblivious to Josh's overactive mind.

Finally, Josh's rattling around in the galley as he searched for coffee, caused Grando yell, "What the hell's going on? Can't a lazy guy get shut eye around here?"

Soon the smell of coffee changed both men's attitudes. Armed with coffee and tea, they began to speculate about what the talk with the islanders might bring. It wasn't long before they noticed their hosts striding along the sandy beach, talking loudly to make sure both men were awake.

The men were dressed in colorful wrap a rounds, which surprised Josh and Grando. Josh offered the three men a cup of coffee and they immediately asked, "What is coffee? Don't you have some of our tea?"

Josh surprised the men by instantly inquiring, "What do you mean, *our* tea?"

With wide grins on their faces, the apparent spokesperson replied, "We have a special tea that grows on the far side of the island, high above on the big mountain. It is prized as a healthy tea. We've been told it would bring in big money if we could sell it to the outside world. We will see that you have a supply before you leave."

The words, "until you leave" were not what Josh wanted to hear. Possible trade, though, opened the opportunity to maybe discuss what Josh had in mind.

To begin with Josh asked their names. Only the spokesman gave his name, which Josh later learned was the traditional way these people dealt with strangers. "I am called Tam Can Do. I go that name because I am the one that makes sure everything gets done on all three of the islands. If you wish, just refer to me as Tam. What are your names?"

Josh the men that the boat belonged to Grando and that he was a helper. "My name is Josh and I've come here from America. Grando lives on the island of Bali. We're friends and business partners."

All three men understood the word friend and it caused smiles all around.

"I think we can understand each other better with Grando's help, so I'll let him do the talking for me. I'd like to learn something about your islands and their people. There are three different islands?" Josh innocently asked.

"Why is it important for you to learn about us? We have been here longer than any other people and have a strong desire to keep out all the bad things the outside world seems to thrive on. Like your love of drink that makes one go crazy and lose direction. We do not approve of things that make the mind go to bad places. I am sure both of you know what I mean."

"I was just curious," Josh said through Grando. "I didn't mean to offend you."

"All right," the spokesman said after hearing the explanation, "I will tell you a little about our islands. Each island serves our needs in different ways and keeps us from depending on anything from the outside. Everything that we want and need the islands and our own hands provide.

"For example, we get our fruit and many kinds of vegetables from the Garden Island, which you can't see from here. Because of the year-round warm weather, we can grow almost everything through all seasons. We also don't get the destructive storms other islands experience.

"There are 346 men, women and children scattered across the three islands. No one is king, emperor, or a lord. We have a manager of sorts, who does almost everything, and that's me. I specialize in making new decisions. That's why I'm called 'Can Do' — I keep the people and important things in their place.

"Many say we are part of a larger continent called Indonesia, which is somewhere over there," he said, pointing in the direction of Bali. "These Indonesian people have never visited our island and that makes all of us very happy.

"We're not fond of visitors here. We are a peaceful society and will not do any harm to anyone even if they should do us harm. That seems to make us a target for unscrupulous men who come here to try to trick us and take advantage of our good nature."

Josh considered what he'd heard, then asked, "Has anyone done you harm recently?"

Tam took a deep breath and stuttered for a moment. "When this happens, it's something we try to take care of ourselves. There is another island about 60 miles east of island number three. Four times a year, people from that island come in long boats carrying clubs and spears. This is some sort of initiation into manhood for their younger men. They rob, rape and even killed our men who try to save their women.

"Supposedly, the young men must take a woman for the first time before he can become a man. We don't believe in killing anything that we do not intend to eat, so it is difficult for us to defend ourselves. This a problem with no answer."

Tam switched to a less depressing subject and started describing the way of life on all three islands. "Our people live in the areas where they contribute most to our community's needs. Thirty-nine other people and I make our homes on Tea Island. We provide the tea, some chickens and a skinny pig when we can catch one. Everyone shares the tea. Included in the total people living there are four children and eleven fine women.

"Because the sea is our main source of meat and some vegetation like seaweed, the residents of Fisherman's Island do all of the fishing. They have three older boats and four men do all of the fishing. Each morning they set out to harvest the catch. When they return, they deliver the fish to each island and pick up fresh vegetables from the Garden Island while they are there, then deliver fish and vegetables to my island. While they're delivering the day's needs, they also make a list of what everyone wants for the next day. It's a simple system but it fits our needs perfectly.

"I think you can see why we don't want or need anything or anyone from the outside world. We've tried to interact several times and it has always led to grief for everyone.

"We're not totally unfriendly. You've been pleasant and wish us no harm, so you are invited to stay here again tonight, but you need to depart tomorrow. If you do so, you'll depart with our friendship and blessings. Do you have any questions?"

Josh was quick to speak up. "Yes. What you've told me about the other island's men and their sick tradition makes me angry. I want to do something about it. These are bad men, who do murderous things to your people and they should be stopped. No one has the right to cause pain and grief to another person or group of people. Is there anything we could do to help? I have a great deal of money at my disposal and could possibly succeed without the use of violence. Who owns those islands?"

Tam spoke very softly. "As far as we are concerned, there is no owner, just the people of the islands. Why do you ask?"

"If all right with you and your people, I want to register some kind of complaint with the politicians in Jakarta. I think they should be made aware of what's going on. It is a known that Jakarta doesn't like freeloaders or people who live off the government and play no part in funding the expense of running a country. As long as you're providing everything you need and not asking them for money, they won't be too interested in visiting you, but they might be willing to do something to discourage the people who've been terrorizing you. I'd like to look into it and see if I can help."

Tam seemed puzzled by Josh's remark and asked, "What can you or those officials do that will stop this?"

"Just agree to let me see if I can get them stopped."

Chapter 11

After that, Josh asked Tam could show them around the Tea Island.

"It will be my pleasure," Tam said. "I will arrange for special treatment for you at our regular evening gathering. Everyone sings and dances. You two will be made to feel most welcome. We don't normally do this for outsiders, but since you want to help us I think I can make an exception.

"We'll begin our tour by taking the trail up through the coconut and banana trees where we'll find the well-used trail that goes to the top of the big mountain. When we're about halfway up, you'll be able to see all three of the islands."

"Do you mind if I take some pictures?" Josh asked. He then had to explain exactly what he wanted to do and show them some digital photos he'd taken earlier.

Tam thought that it was foolish to take a picture when one could see everything from a proper height, but conceded and said, "It is your choice, Mr. Josh."

Josh went on to explain that he was making a record of all the things he saw on this trip. He added that he thought what they were about to see was important and needed to be included in his record.

Tam had no further comments, and they started on their trek. When they reached the midway point, they found a natural stone patio that offered a grand view of the islands. Josh and Grando just stared in disbelief. Looking in all directions, they had the most exhilarating view that either had ever seen.

"Island number two, as you can plainly see, is a giant rock but it has many strong bananas and coconut trees. This island is home to the fishermen, as I said earlier. These people are also our deliverymen as well as doing other needed chores.

"Now, the Garden Island is to your right. From here you can see all the green stuff growing. Each person living on this island takes care of a selected plot of land, tills it and plants what they need. They grow all of the best vegetables native to the islands. The residents share their bounty with the people on the Tea and Fisherman's islands, meaning all are provided for. That's why we don't need or want anything from the outside world."

"That's great," Josh said, marveling at the natives' efficiency.

"Right now, there are about ten fishing boats nearby that don't respect our right to keep them from harvesting everything that lives in our part of the sea. The bay between island number one and number two used to be the most productive bay in all of Asia. That brought the fishing boats with their big nets, and now they've nearly decimated the area. We don't fish there under any circumstances. The ocean is so full of fish in every other direction that we don't have to. We're much smarter about these things than the intruders.

"We don't use money and don't see a need for it. Those men on the big fishing boats don't understand that."

"How do you get the things the islands can't provide," Josh asked.

"Sometimes, we trade with visiting businessmen like your friend, Grando. The fuel boat that visits us from time to time brings what we've asked for, as well, and we trade for what we need by offering them what we grow and the fish we catch.

"Let us return to your boat and we can talk more," Tam suggested.

When they got back to where the trail split in two directions, Tam asked them to stay on the wider trail. "I've got another treat for you," he promised.

As they walked, he began to talk again, "A long time ago, we do not know the exact time, an old man came to our island uninvited and refused to leave. He caused us no problems, so against our better judgment we let him make a place for himself.

"First, he cleaned an area in front of a large cave and began to live there. Within a year, he'd planted some vines that bore a fruit he called grapes. He wanted these all of the grapes for himself, to make what he called wine. He said the people where he came from drank it like water.

"He also used the boat he arrived in to go out and fish the ocean. It was a good boat.

"One morning, we heard a lot of pounding and noise near the bay, a short walk from where your boat is anchored. When we investigated, we found him in the process of building a massive home. How he managed to get all the lumber and other things he needed without us noticing, no one knows.

"Soon he'd built a fine home that seemed quite foolish to all of us. It was far too large and made with thick outside walls and teak wood inside. The floors and much of the furniture was made from the same type of wood. He must've learned about the storms on the island, and made sure everything was sturdy and weatherproof. This area has hurricanes that are extremely destructive.

"When these storms hit, we hide in the caves on the mountain then rebuild our homes when the storm is over. It's an easy process, since our homes are made of large bamboo covered with palm fronds. It's always warm and humid here all year long, and these homes stay cool.

"Let's take the wide path up ahead, then we'll go up a seldom-used path. No one has gone there for many years, so there will be a lot of vegetation in our way."

Tam was right about the green stuff crowding the way. As they stepped over the top of a slight hill, they saw a large building. From the first glance, Josh could feel the strength of the structure. Stepping up on the first steps, it was obvious that heavy wooden planks had been used for all of the construction. The massive three-inch thick doors were not locked.

Josh began to take stock of every inch of the structure. Stepping into the entry he was amazed by the size and wooden interior. To his left was a well-designed combined kitchen and dining area. As he looked to his right, he saw that the room went on for many feet.

He quickly calculated that the room was about 20x30 feet, with a large glass window at the end. This room made a big impression on Josh, and as they were paraded through the remaining part of the house, he didn't pay a great deal of attention to the two large bedroom suites. As they walked out Josh the deep, inset windows had heavy wooden shutters to protect the glass from storms.

"Josh, this is built like a fort and would withstand most anything nature could throw at it. I can't help but wonder how one person was able to build this."

Tam asked if they wanted to take a stroll down to the waterway that separated the Tea Island from Fisherman's Island. "It's an impressive view and allows you to see the bay and the two other islands. There's also a natural swimming area."

When they got there, they saw a pleasant flat, sandy beach facing the narrow area where the sea passed between the two islands. There was a rock sea wall some 90 yards from the edge of the beach. It made for an inviting area.

The wheels were turning in Josh's head. He couldn't help but think about how the whole area was the most beautiful tropical paradise he'd ever seen. He mumbled to himself, "This is much better than Hawaii, and no one seems to know about it."

Josh had begun to formulate his plan to try and impress Tam and all the island people. He knew he could solve their security problem if only he could come live here. *It's going to be an uphill battle to get these people to accept me, but I have to try. This place is perfect.*

They returned to Grando's boat and Tam said that dinner would begin about 30 minutes before sunset. "Just walk up the path where we could see all three islands and keep on the most used path. It will lead you to our village just is beyond the tall coconut forest."

Josh thanked Tam for the tour and let him know how pleased they both were to be allowed to visit such a wonderful, beautiful place. "We'll be honored to join you for dinner. Thanks again."

A short time later, Josh and Grando set out for the village. Before they reached it, both knew that they were close because they could hear Polynesian music and singing as they topped a sandy rise. Both men stopped and beheld the scene before them. It was something most people could only dream about. There were about 20 palm-thatched huts in a semicircle, all facing the channel, looking out to sea. A number of the island people were gathered in the center, enjoying the close of a good day.

"That is the most peaceful get-together I've ever seen!" Grando exclaimed as they looked at the scene.

Josh agreed, as they made their way down to the group. Mr. Tam stepped out to great them as they walked up, and asked all the other people to pay attention. "These two men are our special guests for the evening. They've seen our islands and are impressed with their beauty and peacefulness. Please treat them as our friends; they're different than many who've passed this way.

"The big man is called Josh, and the shorter one is Grando. They live on the island called Bali, some 300 miles south of here. Mr. Josh has said he can help us with the bad island people who keep raiding the Garden Island, and raping our women. We will have a long talk about that and learn just what he has in mind."

The dinner was not typical of the food both men were used to. The ingredients were similar, but the manner of cooking was native to the island people. Different tasty spices had been added and the food was mostly cooked over an open bed of hot coals or in a clay pot. Regardless of how it was prepared, Josh and Grando both enjoyed it immensely.

As the food disappeared, Tam and Josh moved a short distance away from the others so they could talk. Tam leaned close to Josh, and began asking how he was going to help solve their security problem. Tam explained his people had a strong aversion to taking a life when they did not have to. "Killing is the main reason my people left the big island so many years ago.

"At that time, the king felt that he had to destroy anyone he didn't like. Many of the Maori people were against the king but he controlled almost everyone with fear. A small group got tired of the dominance and cruelty of the king and made plans to live elsewhere. All of them crowded into three small boats and headed southwest, not knowing what they might find. They wanted to get away from the fear and find their own peace so badly, that they didn't care where they ended up.

"They had heard of an area south of their location from several traders. It had many small islands and no one lived there.

"After traveling south, they came to a large island that we know now as New Guinea. The people there were unfriendly but they confirmed the location of the islands to the south.

"They continued on their trek and eventually found these islands. No one else lived there, so they decided the belonged to our people. Mr. Josh, that was many, many years ago. From that time forward, other than the island that keeps giving us trouble, we have had no problems and have been visited by only a few traders and fishing boats.

"Now, you're here. For the first time, an outsider wants to help us. I can only hope you mean it and aren't trying to trick us."

Josh hesitated, then said, "Tam, to be honest with you, I'm not sure what I can do. I just know I'm willing to try. I'd like to begin by visiting Jakarta to find out why they haven't helped you and your people. Depending on their response, I'll formulate a plan from there. Are you willing to let me try?

"Yes, I believe you might be able to help us."

"I'd like it if you allowed me to live here and be a part of your community. I won't interfere with your way of life, but I think it will be important for me to be close so that when I figure out what to do to help you, I can do it immediately.

"Mr. Grando and I will go back to Bali tomorrow, and from there I'll go to Jakarta and make a plea for some kind of support. After that, I'll decide the best way to protect your people."

Tam rubbed his short-whiskered chin in deep thought, then said he'd have to speak to his people before he could allow Josh to live with them.

"Tam, I have a question for you before you go. I noticed there aren't many children here. Why is that?"

"About one hundred years ago, the number of new babies was overtaking the ability of the islands to provide. It was a difficult decision, but something had to be if our way of life was to continue.

"After months of discussions, our forefathers came to the decision that only 362 people could be sustained by our islands. Since that time, we have had a firm, but fair means of controlling our population. From that point forward, we only allow a birth when there has been a death. Everyone gathers, and we decide who the next mother will be. This system may seem extreme, but it works for us."

"It works for all of you, so it's the best way for your people," Josh stated.

Tam said there was something else he wanted to discuss with Josh about the Garden Island, but it would have to wait. "I'll reserve that conversation for when the people have decided you can live here. There's nothing to be concerned about, so don't worry."

Chapter 12

Mid-day the next morning, there was a gathering at Grando's boat. The islanders came to say farewell to their new friends. They were hopeful that Josh would find a way to keep them safe.

It was just over 300 miles back to Bali, and the first three days of the trip the sea was as calm as a mirror. The fourth night, just before they got to their home port, the sea became angry. Green water was all they could see, and Josh had to fight to keep his seasickness under control.

Josh had explained what he had in mind for the three islands to Grando as they traveled. Grando just shook his head and told him he was crazy.

The day after landing in Bali, Josh flew to Jakarta and sought out the right person in the Indonesian government. The first person he talked to knew nothing about the three islands. After several more tries, he met a tall, well-dressed gentleman who said he looked after the regulations of all the property that belonged to Indonesia. "What may I do for you?" he asked. "I've heard about what you did in Bali and want to thank you for your help with the needy. My name is Tamara, and I am at your service."

Josh asked if they could find a nice quiet place where they could talk about the serious questions he wanted to ask. "First, Tamara, I want to find out the status of several islands in your sovereign territory." He handed Tamara a slip of paper, and went on to say, "These are the navigation points of the islands in question."

Tamara quickly scanned the paper and called for one of his assistants. He instructed the man to get a map showing all the territories so he could figure out which islands Josh was talking about. The assistant quickly rushed out.

"It will take a few minutes for the map to be located. Can I offer you some refreshment? Have you had lunch?"

"Something to drink would be fine," Josh said.

Tamara led Josh to an opulent room with wooden paneling made of the finest polished teak. Even the desk was made of choice wood. Josh to an equally impressive chair. "I hope you'll call me by my more familiar name, Tee. Tee is the nickname an old family friend gave me when I was young. It seems I enjoyed drinking tea so much that he thought I should be called Tee. It became the family joke and the nickname has stuck with me. So, please, just call me Tee, no mister required. How about you? What should I call you?"

"Just call me Josh, Tee. It's the only name I answer to."

Tee insisted that Josh have dinner with him. "I'll invite several powerful cabinet members to share the evening with us. Maybe we can get something done regarding your request."

The aid came back in the office, and said he had the map but couldn't find the exact islands Josh mentioned.

Laying the map out on the table, he pointed to the area he thought Josh was talking about. Josh moved his finger across the map and stopped where several small dots marked the tiny islands. The area was titled 'Three Islands of Sumwhr.' "This is the area I'm most interested in. Just looking at the map shows how remote the islands are, but they have 362 fine, and self-supporting people living there. They've lived there for hundreds of years. They aren't asking for anything except protection from a neighboring island's men who visit their islands as a rite of passage that involves raping their women."

Josh noted that Tee gave a questioning frown as he asked, "Do they have records that prove they've been on the islands for as long as you say?"

Josh explained that several of the islands' people tradition of passing down their traditions and history orally. It sounds strange to our modern thinking, but many peoples all over the world use oral histories to keep a record of their civilization. The way I was told and what I experienced when I was there leads me to believe they've been there as long as they say."

Since they had time before dinner, Tee suggested that Josh might like to freshen up. Josh responded, "I haven't found a hotel yet. I guess I need to do that first."

Tee told Josh his accommodations had been taken care of. He would be the guest of the state of Indonesia for as long as he needed. Tee called his assistant and had him escort Josh to a bungalow-style apartment at the back of the large complex. The grounds were beautiful and the separate building was quite old but in wonderful shape.

When Josh entered, he found the three rooms to be the same quality as the meeting room he'd just left. Normally Josh would've let out a low level whistle in response to the luxury before him, but he refrained this time. He didn't want to inadvertently insult his host.

After Josh freshened up, he headed off to his dinner date. When he got there, he was sure there'd been a mistake — all of the dinner guests were in full Indonesian attire, which was formal with a strong flash of color.

Tee must have noticed Josh's surprise, because he said, "They like to show off. We don't have many foreign guests. Just wait until they get warmed up, there will not be a stranger in the room. They represent some of the best minds in our country, and there are some fools among them, too. All in all, though, they're good people."

Dinner was far more sumptuous than Josh had expected. There was tray after tray of different meats, fruit and other delicacies he was only partially familiar with. While the food was wonderful, it seemed to Josh that there was far too much blustering going on between the leaders, with them all trying to outdo each other.

Tee leaned over to Josh and said, "This sort of thing goes on at every gathering we have. I think it's called gamesmanship in your country." Josh smiled and agreed.

The rest of the evening was spent with Tee asking questions about the three islands and finding out what Josh's interest in them was. Josh was prepared for this and provided a wealth of information and details. When he was finished, everyone was satisfied but gave no indication of what they would decide.

As Tee slowly walked Josh back to his room, he explained that decisions were never made quickly. "Maybe by tomorrow we'll know more. The fact that the island people do not want any help from anyone was the strongest part of your plea. You must know my country doesn't have a great deal of extra funding for special projects.

"Most of our funding is provided by our oil. We try to treat the production like a money machine, but most of us know it's not an infinite source of income. That's why we like our people to learn to care for themselves, instead of relying on the government to do it. The main stumbling block for your plan is the fact that none of the ministers even knew about these islands before you came to them. I doubt many of them know where they are, even after you told them.

"All that aside, I have a good feeling about this and it is my hope that by noon you will have approval to purchase the islands. The only question will be how much you will have to pay."

Josh was confused. "Tee, what makes you think I want to buy the islands?"

"Josh, your presentation gave us that strong impression. I realize you didn't know you wanted to buy them yet, but I just made your decision easier. How much would you be willing to pay for them?"

"Gosh, Tee, I haven't given that any serious thought. Let me answer you this way. Those three islands have no real value, except to those who now live there. They don't produce enough of anything to sell to the outside world, and they don't use any form of currency. They don't even really understand what money is. The only reason I'd want absolute control of them would be to provide security for the residents.

"I have been in the money world most of my life and know that you're expecting solid numbers. So for the sake of this discussion, I'd offer ten thousand American dollars for each island, that's thirty thousand American dollars total. Would that be an insulting sum?" Josh asked, even though he knew it was a laughable amount.

Tee stroked his beard as he gave it some thought. "Josh, I know the country would end up in another welfare situation if we hold on to those islands, but there are several other issues that need to be considered.

"While you're concerned about the security the three islands, my country has many other greater concerns. What if rogue group attempted to take over? How do you plan to assure Indonesia that you'd do everything within your power to help?"

Josh hadn't thought about that. It was like being responsible for protecting his own little country. "Tee, I don't have an answer for that, since I hadn't even considered buying the islands until a few minutes ago. I need to think about a lot of things if I'm going to take this on. As to your question, I can only promise that I would respond in a very firm way."

"We're having another meeting in the morning, and I will convey your response to the members. Good night, Josh. Have a good night's sleep."

Chapter 13

Tee pounded on Josh's apartment door early the next morning, shouting, "Wake up sleepy head! The day is almost gone and you're still in bed. I want to share a special breakfast with you and one other of our members. Can you meet me in five minutes in the small dining room?"

Josh thought that the loud banging on his door was to impress him that a decision was in the making. Josh was sure that if Tee had known he'd been up for hours and had already showered and shaved, it might have let a little air out of his balloon. So, to keep up the illusion that he was just awakening, he slowly slipped on his shirt and pants and then made his way to the dining room.

When he got there, he noticed there was a huge quantity of food set out for just three men. It looked like more than a small army could devour.

As soon as Josh was seated, hot coffee was poured into his small cup and a server that was at his elbow ready to dish out some of the tasty fruit onto his plate.

He put a healthy amount on fruit on the plate and then asked Josh how he wanted his eggs. Josh just waved him off explaining that he needed to get a cup of coffee down before he could think about food. "Give me a few moments, please."

The conversation at the table was casual and light. Both Indonesian men wanted to learn more about Josh and his life. He gave them the run down on most of his history but left out the details of his original quest. He'd almost forgotten why he started out on this journey. The three islands had been taking up most of his energy and planning for quite some time.

Soon breakfast was finished and the men turned to the business of the day. Tee stood up and said to Josh, "We discussed what you talked to us about yesterday as well as whether we will allow you to buy the three islands. Because you agreed to provide security and keep the residents' best interests in mind at all times, your offer has been accepted. What's your next move going to be?"

Everything had happened so quickly that Josh was at a loss to say. He thought for a moment, and then said, "Tee, since we're talking about me basically buying my own little country here, I think we need to get the lawyers involved. I'll need legal documents that establish my ownership of the islands and clearly state my obligation to Indonesia and our agreement about being involved with each other. Maybe someone on your legal staff could do this? If so, lets get them involved as soon as possible. I need to get back to Bali and set things in motion."

Tee had already thought of this. He picked up a nearby phone and said, "Send them in." Four-well dressed gentlemen rushed into the room immediately. They had with large notepads tucked under their arms and looked ready to get started.

It took most of the morning to complete the legal documents. The legal staff thanked Josh and handed him four copies of the official contract and agreement shortly before lunchtime, and Josh called his bank and transferred $30,000 from his Bali account to the Indonesian government. They all celebrated completing the contract with lunch. Shortly after, Josh boarded a plane back to Bali.

When Josh got back to Bali, he found a note from Hjosan saying the boat company was ahead of schedule and that delivery would be in two weeks. He immediately found a suitable company to do the shipping and notified Hjosan of his selection.

His next task was a fun one — he was going to tell Grando about the new, more powerful boat. He thought that it would be special if he invited Grando to the best restaurant in Bali to give him the good news.

Later that evening, they sat in the restaurant. Grando ordered a double whiskey, and Josh stuck with the local beer.

Josh started the conversation with a review of his friendship with Hjosan. "While I was in Kyoto, Hjosan helped me find the best boat builder in Japan. It just so happens that Hjosan is a close friend of the number-one boat manufacturer and we had an interesting discussion about boats. That's when I decided you needed a brand new boat. I visited the manufacturer and came to an agreement. Your new boat will begin its journey to Bali in about two weeks.

"It's made with heavy aluminum and has double bottoms so that when you 'accidentally run up on rocks, it won't sink. The power will be completely different too. It's got something called a jet drive and uses high-powered water to thrust the boat forward at great speeds. There are no propellers to slice into docks or rocks, which is also a bonus. The engines use diesel fuel, but you'll be able to travel over fifteen hundred miles with out refueling. This boat is my gift to you, dear friend."

When Josh finished explaining, he looked into the weathered face of his friend, and saw that there were tears sliding down his face. "I hope those are happy tears, my friend! I'd hate to think I'd made you cry because you'll have to leave your poor old decrepit boat behind!"

"They're definitely happy! I don't know how to thank you. This is too much."

"Not at all; we're partners. Plus, you don't know the rest of my plans."

Josh shared what happened on his visit to Indonesia and his unexpected ownership of the three islands. "I have to go to the International Court of Justice in the Netherlands to register my new country and try to get it recognized by the UN." After he said this, it finally hit him that he was the sole owner of a country and it shook him to the bone. *Boy, am I in trouble!*

Chapter 14

It was two full weeks before Josh found the courage to book his ticket to the Netherlands. In the meantime, he'd phoned his friend at the U.S. State Department to ask him for a contact on the legal staff of the ICJ. After getting the name, Josh decided to wait until he was there before trying to make an appointment.

The flight involved changing planes twice and fourteen hours of flying time. It was late evening by the time he got to his hotel at the end of the bay of Ijsselmeer. The hotel was old and must've been a beautiful palace of some kind in its previous life. His room was plush and the bed was big enough to hold four people. He arrived too late for dinner in the dining room, but was so tired from the trip that it didn't matter. He went straight to bed so he could be as fresh as possible for this next adventure.

It was Josh's habit to rise early and get ready for the day. He was a little nervous as he dialed the ICJ number and asked to speak to Mr. Vogal.

He was transferred and a gentle voice answered, "This is Reese Vogal, may I help you?"

Josh gave his name and before he could say anything further, Vogal said jovially, "I was expecting your call! What can I do for you? Your friend was vague about the reason for your call."

It sure pays to have friends in high places, Josh thought with relief, then asked, "Could I arrange a meeting to discuss the procedure for establishing a sovereign country? I've recently purchased three islands in the South Pacific from Indonesia."

There was no hesitation in Mr. Vogal's answer. "May I call you Josh? I was expecting your call, but not until later in the week. No matter, I can find the time. What time can you be in my office? Have you had breakfast yet? Possibly we could meet this morning."

Josh said he hadn't eaten yet and Vogal asked, "Where are you staying?" When Josh told him, he said, "Give me a few moments and I'll meet you in the lobby. The restaurant there has some of the best food I've ever eaten, so if you don't mind, we can dine there."

Josh said that was fine and Vogal responded with, "See you in five minutes," then hung up.

I'm going to like this guy, Josh thought. *I like working with people who make things happen quickly.*

After breakfast, Josh and Vogal got ready to get the basics out of the way. Josh reached into his briefcase and brought out the legal documents that established his full ownership of the islands. As he laid out the four copies, he selected the top one and handed it to Vogal, explaining the Global Positioning System data used to pinpoint the islands' locations. "They're somewhere between New Guinea and Borneo."

Reese looked at the information and gave a low whistle. "You own all three islands? What the hell are you going to do with them? I'm afraid you might run into some real problems with neighboring countries."

Reese took Josh's reference to "somewhere" to be the name of the islands and Josh let it pass as he began to finish his own statement, "I own the islands but the people own the land. I have an agreement stating what I'll do for them but it can't really be accomplished until a sovereign state is established along with all the rights and privileges associated with that designation. I can explain further if you need me to, but I really need to know if this can be accomplished. Can you help?"

Vogal said he needed more information, so step by step Josh detailed the content of the agreement and the Indonesian government's contract. He took great pains to make sure each item was understood.

Next, he talked about the great way the island people lived and how their tribes had existed there for hundreds of years and how he became aware of the 362 people who currently called the islands home. He didn't miss any of the details. When he'd finished, he asked, "Do understand why I want to be a part of this and make their lives better?"

"Josh, dear friend, your paperwork is some of the best and most complete I've ever seen. You must've bribed someone to get all that done," he said and laughed.

"Yours is not the first such a request we've received, but this is the first time where only one individual owner is involved. I know one of the things we'll need to know will be how you intend to defend this new country."

"I'll make sure you get all the proper attention by handling this myself. Let's go to my office so I can introduce you to the director of the legal staff. From there, we start to get things set up for you. When we're done, I'd love to visit your country."

Amazingly, it took only two full days before Vogal had everything setup and they could celebrate the successful conclusion of the legal business. Josh was now the proud owner his own sovereign country. He also knew that he was one step closer to his goal for the islands — security and total freedom from fear.

As Josh was reviewing the completed legal documents, he noticed the official name of his country had been listed as The Three Islands of Sumwhr. "Well, I guess that's as good a name as any," Josh said to himself.

Josh had one final request for his new friend Reese Vogal. He asked if the ICJ communicated with most of the countries in the Asian corridor. "Yes we do," answered Reese. "Why do you ask?"

"I want to establish a 25-mile no fishing boundary around my new country. That would be 25 miles from any point of land on each island. This will especially apply to the large bay. This will help to ensure the islanders can remain self-sustaining."

"The islanders have tried to restrict access in the past, but fishermen have ignored them and caused the bay to be nearly fished out. I want to help the islanders restore this area so it can provide for them for years to come.

Vogal agreed to help. He took Josh to the appropriate government office and they filed the paperwork relatively quickly. With that completed, Josh had made the first two steps in protecting his new country and its people.

Chapter 15

Next, Josh traveled to Bangkok, Thailand. Upon his arrival, he decided to book a room at the Sheraton Orchid hotel located near the Chao Phya River. He'd been there before and had considered it a special treat to sit on the balcony and watch the activity on the river. While it had been 10 years since his last visit here, his information was still in their computer and a room near the top of the building on facing the river was is in just a few minutes.

Josh was here to visit an old contact that was an arms dealer. He wasn't sure he'd remembered the guy's name correctly, but he remembered the restaurant he owned. At dinnertime, he hired a driver and a powered car called a Tuk Tuk, similar to a golf cart, and headed to the restaurant.

It took the driver about ten minutes to get to the restaurant. When he entered, Josh asked to speak to the owner. A chubby but colorful man who was all smiles greeted him a few minutes later. Josh had a weird feeling that this friendly looking guy was hiding a deadly side.

Josh introduced himself and asked if there was a quiet table where they could talk. The man immediately lost his friendly smile and led Josh to a dark back room. "What's so important that we need to talk in private?" he asked in a not so friendly manner.

I guess I need to just jump right in, Josh thought. "I need the newest and most reliable shoulder surface to surface missile launchers and missiles that can be had and I need them delivered to a fishing port in Bali. I'm sure that you know how to avoid the officials who frown on such things. I have a boat there, but if the port isn't safe, we can meet you in international waters and make the transfer there. I have money and I'll pay in American dollars. Can this be done? If so, how much will it cost me?"

The dealer gave him a deep scowl and asked, "Are you going to start a war or something?"

"No war, just protection," Josh said. "My people are depending on me to keep the promise I made. I have to keep them safe." Josh went then elaborated on exactly why he needed the weapons.

It was obvious that the weapons dealer didn't believe Josh's story, but it was also obvious that he didn't care why Josh wanted the weapons. He just wanted to be sure he'd get paid. The lure of American dollars was strong. "I will have an answer for you in two days. Are you sure you can pay my prices?"

"That depends on your price. Name it and I can give you half now and the balance upon delivery. There's no reason for you to doubt me, I'm totally serious and have the funds to back it up."

"I'll take you at your word. How many do you want?"

Josh hadn't had time to think everything through and had no immediate response. "Can you supply me with fifty of your newest and best and provide training for their operation? Could you get them tomorrow?"

The tomorrow got a big laugh from the dealer. "Are you kidding? It will take at least four days to get what you want, and then I'll have to make special arrangements for testing and training. Give me five days. I'll contact you."

Josh further surprised the dealer when he asked that he would want maybe fifty more with the same terms at a later date. "Mr. whatever-your-name-is, I'm not fooling around and want to be sure that you can provide the goods."

The "whatever-your-name-is" crack made the guy bristle. "Names are not important in my business. If you have to call me something, then use James, just like your famous Jessie James the outlaw," he said, followed by an evil laugh.

The next morning there was a message at the front desk letting Josh know "the game was on" and he should make himself available in five days. The rest of the mes-

sage read, "That's when I can let you play with the ne
toys." It was signed Jessie James.

There wasn't a whole lot Josh wanted to do in this
city, so he had a Tuk driver take him to the Chinese dis-
trict. He had a fond memory of the place and its tasty
food. He spent the entire day walking around looking
in the various shops. He bought himself a tasty lunch
and continued his window-shopping. Near evening, after
asking a number of shop owners about where he could
find some entertainment, he was told there was a place
at the edge of the city that had the best native Thailand
show. That would be his next stop and where his outing
would end for the day. He had to save something for the
rest of the time he'd be waiting for his meeting.

Five days later, James sent a private car to pick Josh
up and take him to the location where he'd get training
on his new weapons. The location was 30 miles from
downtown Bangkok. The driver didn't say a word as
they traveled, and Josh began to wonder if this had been
a bad idea. The driver finally turned off onto a banana
and coconut tree-lined drive that was anything but flat.

The diver came to a sudden skidding halt near a tin
shack and indicated Josh should get out. When he did,
James stepped out from behind the shack and said, "I
thought you'd got lost. Took you forever to get here. I
have three of the units ready for testing. If you approve,
you'll need to pay." He didn't say anything else, just
motioned for Josh to follow him through the trees. The

vegetation was so thick that when they came to a bend in the trail, Josh couldn't see the drive or the shack anymore.

They eventually came to a clearing where two scrawny looking natives were waiting. Both were barely dressed, but smiled constantly. James went over the basic parts of the launcher and handed it to Josh so he could get a feel for it. After that, James went through the correct steps for setting it up. He went through each step as though the thing was ready to go off at any minute.

Finally, he carefully handed it to Josh and said, "Put the unit up to your shoulder like you would with a shot-gun. Hold it in tight. The correct stance is critical if you want to hit your target."

Josh made the adjustment and James said, "There, just like that. Now aim at that barrel over at the edge of the tree line. Settle in and squeeze the trigger."

Josh followed the instruction and pulled the trigger. There was a loud swish as the missile left the launcher. It was so unexpected that he nearly wet himself. He'd expected a noise but nothing like that! The smoke trail it left was so thick that Josh had to look away from the target. Much to his surprise, when he looked down at the weapon, the barrel was no longer there.

Jessie noticed Josh's surprise and laughed. "The barrel can't be reuscd. It's destroyed it fires. That way it's ready for the next missile."

"Wow, that wasn't as hard as I thought it would be," Josh said.

"Yeah, anyone can do it. That's why they're so dangerous. Will these work for you?"

"I think these will be fine," Josh said. "Name your price and assure the delivery schedule and I'll get you the half payment today."

James wanted the second potential order, so he gave Josh a fair price. Once that was done, Josh also asked about .50 caliber Browning machine guns, and he could almost see James counting the money he'd receive.

With their business concluded, James led Josh back to the shack where the silent driver waited to take him back to his hotel. Josh wanted to get back to Bali and away from all this wheeling and dealing. He was finding out that being the owner of a country was a lot of work. He was exhausted and definitely ready for some R&R.

Josh got back to Bali around noon the next day. When he got there, he couldn't find Grando anywhere. It was almost time for the new boat to be delivered and he didn't want his friend to miss it. Since he couldn't find Grando, Josh headed to his apartment for a long hot, hot shower. As he was toweling off, there was a load roar as Grando came rushing in to greet him.

Once Josh got dressed, he met on the balcony of the apartment and began to explain everything he'd been up to. "I'm the official owner of the country of The Three Islands of Sumwhr. Don't ask how I came up with that name, because it wasn't me! Mr. Vogal instantly put in the name and it sort of stuck. He even spelled it Sumwhr, and that's how it appears on all the official documents. I decided that was as good as any name, and didn't really want to go through the whole process again. So, what the country will be called."

Josh went on to tell Grando about his latest adventure with Jesse James. Grando followed and was somewhat disturbed by the plan to receive the weapons on his boat. "I really don't want to go to jail for this new country of yours," he said, with a worried look on his face.

Josh assured Grando there would be no trouble. "We'll receive them in international waters and I'll make sure to grease some local palms to ensure we get through it without any trouble."

Josh had been so caught up telling Grando about his exploits that he'd completely forgotten about the arrival of the new boat. When he went back inside, he noticed the message light blinking on his phone. The shipping company had left a message saying their cargo ship coming in from Japan was due in to dock the next day. They also gave him shipping cost, which made Josh cringe.

Thinking about finances made Josh realize he really needed an accountant. There were just too many things going on in his life and he couldn't keep track of everything by himself. *The bank in Denpasar has good service, may the bank president knows someone I could use.*

Early the next morning, Josh roused Grando out of a sound sleep and urged him to get dressed. He wanted to go down to the dock and wait for Grando's new boat to arrive. That way they could watch it being unloaded.

When they got to the dock, the cargo boat was already tied dockside and some of the securing lines that held the new boat had already been removed. For the first time, both men got a clear look at the shinny new craft.

"That thing's huge!" Grando exclaimed.

In less than an hour the new boat was sitting in the salt water of the harbor and it had drawn a crowd. Everyone had heard about the new boat and wanted to get a look at it. They all agreed it was one fine looking vessel.

Josh had arranged for a specialist to train Grando so he could keep up with the boat's maintenance. The man, Yuto, found Josh and Grando by asking around, and approached him to find out where he'd be staying. Grando told him that he would share his new apartment with him so that they could get to know each other and have some long conversations about the operation and care for the new boat. Grando admitted he nothing about the boat's systems and would need all the help he could get. Both men seemed pleased at the arrangements.

The next item on the agenda was fueling the boat and getting it started. Yuto demonstrated how to start it up, and the engines made a hollow low roar until he set the throttles to a smooth rumble. The onlookers were quite impressed by this display.

With the two engines warmed, Yuto put the boat in reverse and slowly eased away from the dock, turning the bow of the boat out to sea. As they began to move forward, he explained the jet drive controls to Grando.

Grando found the big blasts of water that shot up from the engines amusing. "Does it do that every time?" he asked, laughing.

Josh stayed on the dock enjoying the way the boat stood out as it moved away from the dock. *That's the best thing I've ever done for a friend,* he thought as he watched the boat all but disappear on the far horizon.

It was a full hour before Josh spotted the tall white spray of bow water as the came tearing back to the dock. Grando was beside himself. He jumped from the boat to the dock, yelling and waving his arms like a crazy man. "Josh! Oh, Josh, that dammed boat hit 45 knots and according to Yuto it still had a lot of throttle left. This boat is something else. Thank you so much!"

"You'll have to earn a part of it, you know," Josh cautioned. "I'll need you to help me keep my promise to the islanders. Your boat is essential to my plans."

"Oh, I know that, my friend. It's still the best thing ever!"

"I'm so glad you like it, Grando. I think I'm going to head to my apartment so I can make a list of all the things we'll need to take to the islands. I'm going to have to get organized. If I don't, I have no idea how we'll ever be able to do everything I want to accomplish.

"That big house needs cleaned and some major improvements need to be made, like running water, electricity and an indoor bathroom. The plumbing issues are a big cause for concern. The list goes on and on. I guess I'll have plenty of time get things fixed up once I get there. I also bought two high quality radios so we can keep in touch once I'm living there full time."

Grando had a blank look on his weathered face. "Do you mean that we're going our separate ways, dear friend? I don't think I'll like that."

"Grando, we will always be friends and we'll see each other all the time. I'll need all sorts of building supplies and other things, and I'd hoped you'd be the one to procure them and bring them to me. Of course, you'll always be a welcome guest and you can stay for as long as you like. We'll build a nice dock so you'll have a secure place to leave the boat."

Grando still had that lost look on his face, but agreed they'd figure out a way to make it work.

Chapter 16

Josh spent the next five days in his apartment making a long list of what he thought he would have to have as soon as he moved permanently to The Three Islands of Sumwhr. There was a lot to consider and plan for and he tried to be thorough.

The day before the weapons were due to arrive, Josh and Grando went over the plan for receiving the merchandise. They decided they would meet the boat 40 miles out at sea, where there'd be no chance of government to interference. Grando was very nervous but Josh assured him they'd stick to the plan and no one would even see them.

Finally reassured, Grando asked if they could go to their favorite restaurant and have a pleasant quiet dinner. Josh quickly agreed and volunteered to pay.

By midnight, the last of the items Josh had packed to take to the islands were packed away on the boat. They were ready for their trip the next day.

Before the sun was up, both men were on the boat. A short time later, the boat quietly slipped out of the harbor, it's bow pointed due north. They ran at about fifteen knots for an hour before a radar blip showed up on the screen. Josh warned Grando that they had to be cautious because they were dealing with some scary men.

Josh looked through his powerful binoculars and spotted the boat just coming over the horizon. It looked like the ship they were looking for. After some careful maneuvering, both boats came together and tied up side by side. The captain of the cargo boat asked if Josh was on board, then said Jessie James had a present for him.

Within minutes, the fifty boxes were loaded into the forward compartment and Josh handed the captain a sealed envelope that contained a bank draft for the balance of the agreement. With that done, both boats put their engines into high gear and parted ways.

"See, Grando, I told you we'd have no problems."

Grando set the GPS for The Three Islands of Sumwhr then sat back in the captain's chair and said, "We should arrive at your country in about 15 hours."

Since they had a lot of time on their hands before they reached their destination, both men eased down into comfortable chairs on the deck and dozed off. Neither had had much sleep the night before and would need to be alert when they got to the islands.

When they got there, Tam was met them at the makeshift dock on island number one. He stood out as the most important person and was waving his arms as the boat docked.

"Mr. Josh and Grando, welcome back my friends! We've been most anxious for your return. Have you completed your plans to keep our islands secure?"

"Tam, I have a great many surprises for you all, but first, come join us on Grando's new boat. There will be three more boats just like this one on their way here soon. I bought them for the island fishermen to use. I'm so happy to be back here and I intend to make my home here."

The three men sat on the warm after deck of Grando's boat after Tam had taken the grand tour. Josh began to unfold a bunch of serious looking papers, then said, "Tam, the plan I came up with might seem extreme to you and your fellow islanders, but I assure you this is the only way I could find to make sure you are all safe." Josh went on to explain that he'd purchased all three islands and declared them a new country called The Three Islands of Sumwhr.

At first Tam scowled, but as Josh went on to further explain that he owned the islands, but the people owned all the land, he looked more hopeful. By the time Josh finished his explanation, Tam had a big smile on his face.

"Now that you're our leader, what about the problem with them plundering and raping our women?" Tam asked.

Josh asked Tam to follow him and they went to the area where the missile launchers and missiles were stored. "Unfortunately, force is the only real answer I could come up with. These are shoulder held missile launchers. These should be enough to convince the bastards they don't need to come back! That, or they'll put them in their graves."

At the mention of graves, Tam frowned and said, "Do you mean to kill them?" We're totally against taking a life. Don't you remember? I don't think the people will approve of your solution. I'll need to better understand what you intend to do if I'm to persuade everyone to go along with your plan. Can you give me enough information so I can make a good argument?"

Josh went back to the very beginning of their association, when Tam had expressed told him about the problem. "None of you will have to do the dirty work. I'll do it for you. Of course, I'll try to convince them the non-lethal way first, but if they don't cooperate then I have every intention of blowing them up. I don't like this solution either, but if you and your people are ever going to be truly safe, this is the only way to stop them. Does that make sense?"

After a full minute, Tam shook sadly and said, "I guess it has to be this way. I will make the people understand. What do you need us to do?"

"Well, the first thing we need to do is unload these weapons.

"I know just where we can put them," Tam said. He went on to explain the cave that could be seen from the bay was large and dry and would make a great storage area.

A short time later, the weapons were safely stored in the cleanest part of the cavern. As they finished up, Josh began to tell Tam about his plan for the abandoned house, and why he needed help from the islanders to make it happen. "I'll draw up some plans and then explain them to anyone who wants to help. I'll also need help unloading my supplies."

"I'll get some men to help with the unloading right away," Tam said as he headed off to talk to his people. In no time, there were five men working to unload the boat.

When all the boxes were on shore, they started carrying them to the house. With so many men helping, it didn't take long to get everything moved into the house. When it was finished, Josh stretched his arms wide and said, "I'm really going to feel at home here!"

Later, everyone on the island was seated around the fire, enjoying their evening meal. When they'd finished eating, Tam stood up and asked for everyone's attention. "As all of you now know, Mr. Josh has returned with the answer to our security problem with our neighbors who keep causing us much grief. His solution won't make you happy, but he assures me that none of us will have to be involved. He also found a solution to stop outside fishing boats from invading our fishing areas.

"To do all of this, though, Mr. Josh had to buy our islands and create a new country called The Three Islands of Sumwhr. Before you get upset, he assures me that while he may own the islands, we will own the land and can do with it what we wish. He does not wish to change our way of life in any way other than to make it safer for us to exist.

"Every decision about the way the land and sea is used will be ours. If we decide to grow more crops, it will be our decision. If we decide to fish more, that will be our decision too.

"Mr. Josh intends to live here with us in the abandoned house. He wants to make some improvements there and would like to know if any of you will help him with that. I've already told him I will help.

"Are we all agreed that he can live here and help us with our problems? He seems to be an honest and straightforward person and I completely trust what he has told me. I vote that he be allowed to live here with us. Anyone else have anything they'd like to say before we vote?"

No one said anything against Josh. Since there was only silence in response to his question, Tam called for a vote. The islanders unanimously agreed to go forward with all of Josh's plans, as well as letting him live there with them.

Throughout the following morning and the rest of the day, Josh and Grando worked at unpacking what Josh had brought. The house was full of dust, sand and all sorts of creepy crawlies. They swept and scrubbed and cleaned until the house gleamed. Finally they got to the last of the unpacking, the fresh bedding, toiletries and all the things needed to outfit the kitchen.

While they worked, the fishermen delivered a large supply of shrimp and flounder. After all their hard work, both men were starving. They made quick work of preparing the bounty for the first meal in Josh's new home. They ate until they were uncomfortably full, then quickly did the dishes.

They sat down in the living room and Josh set about making sure that Grando knew he could do whatever he wanted at this point. If he wanted to stay and help with the islanders' issues, he was welcome. If he wanted to go back to his regular business, Josh was fine with that too.

"Grando, you'll need to decide what you want to do and how involved with all my plans you'd like to be. I know I'll have to travel to Japan for supplies soon, and I also need to find an engineering company in Australia to get some plans together to make that cave a true storage facility for the weapons. I probably also need to find a geologist to evaluate the structure of the cave.

"The first thing I need to do here at the house is find a way to have electricity. I've also noticed steam vents around the island. I'm hoping these can be utilized to run a generator. I really won't need much. Just enough for the small radio, some lights and a way to pump water here, and then some lights at the cave."

"Then, all the loose rock has to be removed and pushed into the edge of the bay just outside of the cave.

A large limestone patio could be made here at the front so we have a level place to just sit and admire the surroundings. I'd also like to make a small landing strip so I can get an amphibious plane. If I'm going to travel to Japan and other places all the time, I'll need faster transportation than your boat. Plus, I can't expect you to ferry me around everywhere.

"I had a pilot's license a long time ago, but haven't flown for years. I'm sure I can brush up on my skills pretty quickly. If I get a water plane, we won't have to finish the landing strip any time soon. I can just leave the plane on the water for now.

"As you can tell, I have so darn much whirling around in my head that it's hard to settle on what to do first! Grando, I need your help and suggestions as often as possible. Would you mind being my sounding board?"

"I'll help you any way I can, my friend. I'll also try to keep you from doing something stupid," Grando said and laughed.

Chapter 17

Grando spent the next two days helping Josh, then told him he had some things he needed to do. "I'll be back as soon as I get them done," he said and headed to his new boat. When he was about fifty miles away, he turned on the radio to make sure it worked. At first it made a short crackling noise then hummed as it found the base frequency. "Hello, Josh," Grando said. "I'm about fifty miles from you now. Do you hear me?"

A reply came through with Josh saying, "I hear you just fine. Have a good journey home. I'll call you later this evening."

With Grando gone, Josh began a list so he would know what needed to be done first. He and the islanders made quick work of several things he listed and the days went by quickly.

Two weeks after Grando's exit, Tam came running up to Josh's house and shouted, "Three canoes are coming around the west end of island number two! There are five men in each boat. They'll be here within the hour."

For a second, Josh stood as frozen. Then quickly he snapped out of it and rushed to the cave to grab the missile launcher and two missiles. He ran to the spot where he could see the enemy as they made their way to the beach. He set the weapons down and ran back for two more missiles.

Each missile weighed twenty-six pounds and they weren't the easiest things to carry. He set the second two missiles about a hundred feet to the left of the first two, then slid the first two out of their boxes and set them near the area where he wanted to fire them.

As the canoes came into sight, Josh was awed by the majesty of the tall, half-naked man standing in the bow of a canoe. He held a spear at the ready in his right hand and was waving it in a threatening way. Josh stopped staring and shouldered his weapon.

When the first canoe was about thirty yards from the beach with the second a short distance behind, he sighted the scope on the mid section of the lead canoe and squeezed the trigger to the first detent. Almost immediately, the red laser circle glowed in the site, telling him he was on target. Josh took a deep breath and pulled the trigger to the second detent, just as he'd been taught. There was a loud swish as the missile released and his sight was blocked by the smoke trail. He was almost afraid to see if he'd hit the target.

He quickly picked up the second missile and fired at the second canoe. His peripheral vision let him know that the first canoe was completely gone except for some debris floating on top of the water. When the second missile hit, he saw the second canoe literally jump into the air and explode into tiny pieces. The commotion had alerted the sharks and those who had survived the missiles weren't long for this world.

Josh had a heavy heart. Taking lives didn't come easily for him. When the full weight of his actions hit him, he couldn't stomach it and promptly threw up.

When his stomach was finished revolting, he turned and looked at Tam, who was staring back in complete fear.

"That was… You have killed all those people!" Tam wailed in despair.

The third canoe escaped damage and had quickly turned to make its escape. The warriors' paddles were digging deep into the water propelling them as fast as possible.

Josh, resigned to finishing his mission, shouldered the third missile, took aim fifty feet behind the fleeing canoe and fired the missile. It struck the sea just where he'd intended and caused a gigantic column of salt spray.

Turning to Tam, Josh explained that he wanted to be sure he'd made his point to the remaining men so they would relay the message to the rest of their tribe. "Hopefully they'll be too afraid to come back. That will truly put an end to your problems with them."

Tam and Josh sat down on the sand and stared at the spot where ten men had just died. Both had deep feelings of regret. Josh, with tears streaming down his cheeks, turned to Tam and said, "It had to be done. If we hadn't sent the message to them in a language they understand — violence and death — then they'd be back with reinforcements and your problems would multiply. This way, they know you mean business and I don't think they'll challenge you again. Believe me, I didn't do this thing lightly."

The remainder of the day and evening found all the islanders in a somber mood. They'd learned what Josh did to protect them. While they were glad to be safe, none of them were happy that their safety came at a cost of human lives. Eventually, some of the women came to Josh's house to thank him for ending their fear. This helped Josh to know that his solution had been the correct one.

As the evening wore on, Josh found a spot on his deck and sat looking out to sea. He let his mind drift where it wanted to go and came to terms with what he'd done. As he sat there thinking, he realized that no matter what he'd done, life would go on and tomorrow would be another fine day in this island paradise.

He decided to take a walk to the far west end of his domain. There was no path, just soft white sand. He enjoyed looking at the many tall, graceful coconut trees as he walked toward the sea. He'd only visited this area once before, but knew it was a special place. When he reached the water's edge, there was an old cocoanut tree that had fallen over but was still alive. The main part of the trunk was just a few feet above the sand and it had bent so that it made a seat. *How convenient,* Josh thought. *This is just the right place to sit and gaze out at the sea.*

The sun was in its finest glory and high thunder-clouds stood bright and white against the colorful sky as it set. He sat there until the last of the fading sun sunk into the sea and he was immersed in twilight. *It's time to head home and find something for dinner.*

Nine days after what Josh had come to call "the missile incident," the alarm bell rang from Fisherman's Island. Josh immediately ran to the cavern to collect the launcher and several missiles. As he was doing this, three of the men from Tam's village came running to join him. The men excitedly told Josh there were five canoes headed their way, each carrying several men "They are waving killing clubs and chanting something that we don't understand," one of the men said quickly. "They sound angry."

They ran to the same spot where Josh had fired the missiles last time. The canoes were just rounding the west part of island number two and Josh agreed with the men's assessment — they definitely angry.

Josh asked the men bring him two more missiles from the cave. Josh guessed there were thirty-five or forty men in the five canoes. He was going to have to move fast to do something about their approach; he couldn't let them reach land. Gesturing to the men who were headed back from the cave, he told them to hurry and unpack the missiles as soon as they reached his position.

The first two canoes were beside each other, and Josh aimed for the space between them; hoping he'd get two for one. It took him only seconds to arm and fire the second missile. Just as fast, he began reloaded and attacked the third and then fourth canoes. Each missile found its target and sent wood and men flying. The fifth canoe didn't even attempt to turn. It's rowers dug their oars in with renewed vigor, trying to reach land before Josh could blow them out of the water. They bent their heads low, like they could duck the missiles, and continued to rush toward land.

Josh aimed and fired at the last canoe. He watched as the missile tore the canoe apart, flinging the occupants into the sky, then dropping them into the bay where the sharks waited to greet them.

Josh turned to the men, expecting to see regret on their faces, but he was amazed to see stoic resolve instead. Josh walked over to the three men and said softly, "They were determined to kill all of us. It was a matter of self-defense and we have nothing to regret. The number of men we just eliminated must mean there are very few left on their island. It's my hope we won't be bothered by them again."

As Josh looked around, he realized Tam wasn't with them. "Where's Tam? He should've been witness to the end of this terror. I'd best go find him."

Josh found Tam sitting under his favorite coconut tree with tears streaming down his face, "You should be smiling, not crying. You and your people have nothing left to fear from that tribe."

"You've stopped them, but it came at a terrible price. I will never be happy about taking lives. I just hope your solution for dealing with the fishermen who invade our territory will not be so deadly."

"Most of the fishermen will abide by the sovereign law, so we won't have to worry about them. The few who ignore it will be dealt with when the time comes. Of course, we can try to persuade them in non-violent ways to honor our boundaries, but if they refuse … I'm afraid we'll have to demonstrate our firepower once again. I can always fire warning shots. If that doesn't work, though, I'm afraid the solution is to become more violent."

"Josh, killing will always bother all of us. Even though none of the islanders actually fired the missiles, we still feel responsibility for the deaths. I realize we will just have to accept this and go on. We do worry that if all the men from the other island were eliminated how will the women and children survive. Doesn't that bother you, Mr. Josh?"

Josh hadn't thought about that. "I guess we should go check on them," Josh told Tam.

He and Tam went to find the best fishing boat's crew, and asked if they would go to the invaders' island. The men were all quick to volunteer for the trip.

As the dawn came the next morning, Tam, Josh, and the fishing boat's crew climbed aboard the boat and headed south to the invaders' island. "If we did kill all their men, we'll need to show them how to plant gardens for vegetables, harvest fruit and teach them how to fish. It may take a while but I'm sure that the women will be up to the task," Josh said.

When they got to the island, they learned they truly had eliminated all of the men from this tribe. While the women were wary of the people who'd killed their men, they also knew they needed help to survive. An uneasy truce was established and several of the men from the fishing crew agreed to stay for a while to teach the women what they needed to know.

Chapter 18

A few days after returning from what Tam's people were referring to as "The Island of the Ladies," Josh decided he'd better make a list of his priorities so nothing important would slip through the cracks. The first thing on his list was building a dock so the new fishing boats would have a secure place to tie up. *The boats are going to be delivered soon, so I'd better get busy on that,* he thought.

The Australian engineers would also be returning soon to finish the construction on the cave. *It will be nice to have the weapons secured. That space might also come in handy during severe storms,* Josh mused.

The last thing he thought about was supplementing the food supply for the islanders. *I think a few pigs and some chickens would do that nicely. Now I just have to convince the islanders to try something new. Well, there's no time like the present,* Josh thought and headed out the door to find Tam.

Tam saw Josh walking toward him with a frown on his face, and asked, "What's bothering you on such a fine evening?"

"Would you mind sitting down with me so we can discuss some things I've been thinking about?"

Tam agreed, and they took a seat under one of the coconut trees. Josh proceeded to talk to Tam about his idea for bringing in some pigs and chickens. "These animals don't require specialized food — they eat just about anything. They would be a great source of food and would mean you wouldn't have to rely so heavily on fishing to feed your people."

Josh reminded Tam that the Australian engineers were coming back soon. "If you agree, I'll have the animals brought in and the engineers can design pens for them so they don't run around everywhere all the time."

"We'll try these new animals and see what happens. I can't guarantee the people will like eating them, but there's no harm in trying."

With that settled, Josh moved on to the next item on his list of things to do. "I'm sure you know the new fishing boats are due to arrive any day now. My problem is we have no safe place to dock them. Could you and some of the other islanders decide the best place for a dock? While the engineers are here, we can ask them to draw up plans for a dock as well. We need to be sure we have a place to shelter the boats and tie them down during a storm."

"I will gather some of the fishermen. They'd be the best ones to talk to about this. When they've decided on a location, I will let you know."

They concluded their talk and went their separate ways.

That evening, Josh joined the village for dinner. Tam asked him to sit at his side so they could talk as they ate. "Many of the people have asked me why you live alone. There are several ladies here who would like to keep you company. As you know, there are twenty women to each man here; the women all think it's a waste for you to be alone.

"Maybe you'd allow me to arrange some interviews for you? It would make everyone happy to see you with someone."

Josh had a look of pure fear on his face. Then he started thinking about the women on the Island of Ladies and how they made him feel happy. None of them made him feel trapped or uncomfortable, as many of the women in his life had previously. When he realized Tam was waiting for an answer, he said, "I haven't thought about having a woman in my life. I don't know, maybe it *would* be nice to have someone, but now is not the time. I have too much to do.

Tam knew he'd pushed Josh as far as he could on this subject, so he switched topics and started a discussion about bringing in chickens and pigs. His fellow islanders surprised him by agreeing to this new addition to their food supply without an argument.

Chapter 18

arly in the morning two days later, there was a loud noise coming from the bay side of Tea Island. Josh had been enjoying some of the island's best tea and hadn't noticed the steamer ship slowly approaching. The loud sound had been the ship's horn, announcing its arrival. "Oh shit!" Josh shouted. "The new boats are here!"

The horn had awakened every one on all three islands and soon all of them jumped into their fishing boats and came flying to the Tea Island's beach. Josh had briefly explained how the boats were going to look but sitting on the aft deck of the transport ship, they looked huge. Shortly after the transport ship dropped anchor, the first of the new boats was dropped into the salt waters of the bay. The second boat took even less time to unload.

The two first boats were routine fishing boats, but the third was designed to capturing the many different species to restock the bay. Josh didn't know much about marine biology but he knew the bay was one of the most productive marine nurseries in the greater South Pacific. Repopulating it would fulfill one of his promises to the islanders. Fishing wouldn't be allowed in the bay from this point forward, so it could heal itself and repopulate.

When the last boat was in the water, Josh gathered the fishermen and began to explain what the third boat would do, "The large tank that covers most of the back of the boat is for holding the fish and other marine life we find so we can bring them back to the bay. Seawater is pumped through the tank at all times, in order to keep the fish alive. I think we should go out looking for marine life one day each week until we're satisfied that the bay is on its way back to good health. I hope some of you will help me with this.

"This boat also has no propellers. The drive system pulls seawater in and blasts it out at a greater speed, and that's how the boat is propelled through the water. Since there are no propellers, you won't have to watch for debris and rocks when you're just fishing in this boat. It is also much faster than any of your older boats."

The men were excited about the new boats, and Josh was pleased with what he'd done. *That's one more thing I can mark off of my to-do list,* he thought.

Josh had arranged for an expert to train the fishermen. He would teach them both how to operate the boats and how to maintain them. The most difficult task Josh faced during this time was keeping the islanders from using the boats before they'd learned how. Every one of them wanted to try the new toys immediately. Tam helped with restraining their enthusiasm, and eventually everyone was paying attention to the training.

It took a long time to answer all the islanders' questions. Finally, they were ready for live demonstrations. They boarded one of the boats and the expert started the engine and put the drive system in gear. The force of the water being forced from the drive made everyone on the beach take a step back, but it didn't dull their enthusiasm.

After several hours, it was time let each fisherman try his had at operating the boat. Each vessel was fifty feet long, and charged across the waters making very little noise. Each man reveled in the experience of being the captain for a while.

The boat finally returned after every man had taken a turn. The whole group then came ashore. When they arrived, Tam got everyone's attention and announced that Josh was giving the three boats to them as a gift. There was a roar of approval at that announcement that brought a smile to Josh's lips.

After that, people return to their work and things were back to normal. The fishermen, however, continued to appraise their new boats. Josh could tell they were eager to get the boats loaded with gear and go out fishing.

The third boat, with the tank, required a simple exchange of information with everyone who would be involved with restocking the bay. Filling the large tank, and how to empty it with whatever they had stored in it was a challenge. It had to be done carefully to ensure the catch stayed alive.

As they were about to conclude the demonstrations on the third boat, Grando came speeding around the west point of Fisherman's Island. When he came ashore, he looked over at the new boats and jokingly asked, "How come I only got one?"

Shortly after, the trainer boarded the cargo ship. As soon as he was aboard, the ship's horn sounded once again and it slowly steamed out to sea.

That evening the meal was more entertainment than food. Josh had a long talk with the fishermen and told them it would be best if all of them went out on one boat for a few days until they got used to how everything worked.

Chapter 19

Three uneventful weeks passed after the boats were delivered. The only thing that happened was the arrival of the Australian engineer. This morning, Josh was headed out to find the man to discuss the design for the animal pens. He'd finally come to the conclusion that he had no idea what was needed for this project and was more than willing to let the engineer decide.

He also wanted to discuss the plans for the cave. He'd decided an office/living space — maybe three rooms or more — would be a nice addition. He was spending more and more time there and it would be nice to have everything he needed there, so he could even sleep there if he wanted to. It was a long walk from the cave to the house, especially in the dark.

While he'd been thinking, Josh's feet had taken him to the cave. He went in and started looking at the available space. There's room for a bedroom, bathroom and shower with no problem, he thought, swiping his hair out of his eyes. It had become quite long since he'd left civilization.

The radio crackled and the voice of the Captain of the Australian ship that was bring the huge doors for the cave announced they were less than a day away. Josh was glad the crew would handle unloading the doors, that way he didn't have to worry about the islanders hurting themselves doing work they weren't used to.

When the large ship arrived the next day, Josh saw it had bow doors that swung wide open so large items could be unloaded with ease. The ship's Captain maneuvered the ship so that the bow was close to the beach near the cave. Like a bunch of ants, the workmen came rushing out of the ship.

The foreman of the work crew hired to install everything Josh had ordered approached and asked Josh, "Where do you want it?" Josh pointed to the dark opening of the cave and told him that's where the doors would be installed."

The foreman explained there were several things to be done before the doors could be installed. "The plans I was given show the base and the overheard rails that hold the doors have to be installed first on the left. Then, and only then, can we attach the doors."

He went on to say he understood that they needed to stick to the area around construction site and not disturb any of the natives. "We have plenty of food but we hoped you'd provide some fresh vegetable, fish and other seafood to help supplement what we brought. Would that be possible?"

"I'm sure I can arrange something for you by the end of the day," Josh told him.

When they finished talking, the foreman went to supervise unloading everything. As the giant doors of the ship opened, several heavy cranes were driven out. Next came three large front loaders with four-wheel trailers behind them. The trailers contained all the fasteners and special tools needed for the installation.

When the work was well underway and everyone looked like they knew their jobs, Josh approached the foreman to see if he'd agree to do the additional work he had in mind. "Can I talk to you when you can spare a few minutes? I need to ask you about some additional work I'd like done. You might be able to do part of it on this trip, but the rest will probably require an additional visit."

Josh chose to talk about the shelters first, taking the foreman up the slight hill to where he intended to put the animal pens.

After checking all of Josh's specs the foreman let him know that at least one of the front loaders would be available to work on this project part of the time. "He can do the excavation work, but you'll have to arrange for someone else to do the actual construction. I can recommend someone if you like, he's my wife's brother. Just let me know if you want his contact information."

"That's great. Give me his information and I'll go see him as soon as I can."

Josh knew he couldn't delay, since he'd already arranged for the animals. He called Grando and asked him if he would take him to Bali so that he could fly to Australia. Grando agreed, and Josh made all the arrangements.

When he'd finished, he told the foreman what he'd planned. The foreman said he'd contact his brother-in-law and ask him to meet Josh when he arrived. He handed Josh several phone numbers and the address of his brother-in-law's business. Josh felt better, since he was one step closer to crossing this off his to-do list.

Chapter 20

A couple of days later, Grando came to pick Josh up and take him to Bali. "I needed to get back soon," he told Josh. "I've got some important business to take care of."

Josh grabbed his bag and the two headed to the boat. When they were both onboard, Josh said, "Shove off, Captain," and chuckled. Grando took him seriously, speeding off to their destination at full throttle.

Josh had to stay overnight in Bali, since his flight to Australia wasn't until the next day. He had to change planes in Darwin, a city on the North end of the country.

The foreman's brother-in-law lived in Melbourne. The city was interesting, and Josh knew that he was going to enjoy his stay. He found a hotel near Port Phillip Bay. Josh's room was spacious, and overlooked the bay. The view from his room gave him an almost 180 degree view of most of the city.

After he'd got settled in his room, he phoned the engineer, Robert Ainsley, who answered the phone with a friendly voice. Josh didn't have to explain what he wanted. Robert told him he knew exactly what was needed.

Robert seemed to be more excited to learn about Sumwhr than the potential business, so Josh indulged his curiosity. Robert invited Josh to dinner that evening, saying they'd have a tasty steak at one of the best restaurants in town. Josh's mouth watered at the thought. It had been a long time since he'd had a steak.

Josh enjoyed talking to Robert and hoped he'd be interested in doing the work on the island. He let Robert know he would stick around as long as needed to get all the specifics nailed down. As they ended the evening, Robert invited Josh to breakfast the next day.

When Josh got to the restaurant the next morning, Robert had already ordered steak and eggs for both of them. When they'd finished breakfast, Josh showed Robert his rough drawings for the two shelters he wanted built for the animals.

When they'd finished discussing the drawings, Robert asked Josh to tell him about how he came to be the owner of his own country. Josh told him about his time in New York City, then about his quest to find a country where he could make a difference. He quickly spoke about his friend Grando and how they worked together.

"By chance, I've finally found a small group of people who just want to live their lives and aren't looking for a handout. They live an idyllic life, and only had a few needs they couldn't satisfy themselves. I'm helping them with those needs and they've given me a beautiful place to live."

Robert sat there mesmerized during Josh's story, then said, "That's the most interesting story I've ever heard."

"Now that you know my life's story, how about we get back to work?" Josh asked with a chuckle.

Turning over the sheets of Josh's rough drawings Robert commented that they were really detailed. "I don't know much about pens and shelters for chickens and pigs, but I know some people who specialize in that sort of thing. I think we should go talk to them, since they aren't that far away."

"Sounds like a plan," Josh said.

The time they spent talking to the animal pen specialists was an eye opener for both men. Josh even got some pointers about what breeds would work best for the island. When it was all said and done, Josh had refined the details on his drawings and Robert was sure they had everything they'd need to start construction.

Robert invited Josh to dinner again that evening. "We've had such a successful day and I'm looking forward to working on your projects," Robert said. "Tonight's dinner is on me."

The next day Josh and Robert worked on the plans for the rooms in the cave. Josh mentioned that he still hadn't figured out how to generate electricity for the cave and house. "I have a steam driven generator, but it's still sitting inside the cave. The engineers told me I need to drill deep holes into the volcanic vent and then pipe the steam to the generator," Josh told Robert. I think I have all the components to make it work, but I might need your help with that too. For now, I've got a small diesel generator to run the basics, but that's not going to cut it in the long haul."

"When we get there, I'll see what I can do for you," Robert said confidently.

"Well, the next thing on the list is some sort of septic system," Josh said. "That and a way to get clean fresh water where I need it. I've got a feeder line that comes down from a lake up on the mountain. It would be great if we could get water installed in some of the islanders' homes as well as at the cave and my home."

Robert said he had an idea for the septic system. "It's a closed system used primarily in Europe and on large passenger ships. Everything goes into a separator and the liquid is recycled and purified, then returned to the sea. The solids go into a system where they become just a small handful of compost material. Nothing is returned to the environment in its original form.

"I think that type of system might be what you're looking for. If you want, I can get all the information for you."

Josh smiled and thanked Robert for looking out for his best interests.

Chapter 21

By the fifth day, the draftsman had completed the formal designs for all of Josh's projects. The three of them spent an evening going over every detail to make sure everything was correct. When Josh said the drawings were were perfect, Robert asked Josh to sign off on the projects so he could begin to gather materials and find workers to do the job.

"I'd like to have everything on the dock and ready to go by the end of next month," Josh said. "That's only 43 days. Will that give you enough time?"

"Because your location is so remote, I'll have to have everything I need before we leave. That's going to take some major planning on my part. I think we can get it done on schedule. I'll let you know if something comes up and we can't do it that quickly."

Josh was pleased with everything they'd accomplished and thanked Robert for his expert assistance. "I'm going to take a flight back to Bali first thing in the morning. I still have a lot to do. I think you should plan for a minimum of 15 days to do the work. While you're there, I'd be happy to give you a tour of my country if you like."

"I wouldn't have it any other way," Robert said. "After everything you've told me, I can hardly wait to see the place."

Josh thanked Robert again and headed to his hotel to get things packed up. This flight was an early one, and he didn't want to leave anything until the last minute. While he was packing, his cell phone rang. The number wasn't familiar, but he answered anyway.

"Josh I heard you were here. Why haven't you called me?" Frank Peters, the Australian petroleum engineer who was testing some samples from the bay that Josh had sent a month ago, demanded when Josh answered his phone.

"It's a good thing you called. I've been so busy with everything else that I'd almost forgotten about the samples."

"Well, the guy you need to talk to is named Olen Roach. He's the head of the Australian Petroleum Research Institute or something like that. He seemed really excited about talking to you. I think we should get together soon and talk about what he found."

"How about in an hour?" Josh asked. "Tell me where to meet you, and I'll be there."

An hour later, the engineer was standing on the curb as Josh's taxi drove up.

"Hi, Josh," Frank said as Josh got out of the taxi. "Olen is waiting for us in his office."

It was a short walk to Olen's office and Frank was almost shouting at Josh all the way over. When Josh asked what had him so excited, he said, "Just wait. Olen will tell you all about it."

Olen was standing in front of a stack of papers that covered his desk when they walked in. "Josh Crammer, am I ever glad to meet you," Olen said. "I have good news and great news to share with you. Let's get out of this mess and have a cup of coffee. I think that you'll need some kind of stimulant after you hear what I have to say."

"What's all the fuss about? Have I won the lottery or something?"

For the next hour, Olen and Frank double-teamed Josh with all the information about the sample he'd sent them. Apparently it was oil.

"Ralph tells me that the bay that is the main part of your country, which by the way has a really weird name. What's the story behind that?"

Josh, not wanting to spend the day retelling how he became the owner of a country, put Olen off by asking for more details about the oil.

"First, we have no idea how much oil is there. We'll have to do more exploration before we can figure out an estimate and what we'll need to drill for it. I suspect the drilling will have to be done with deep-water drilling rigs. Australia is home to three experienced companies do this type of exploration in Indonesia and the surrounding country. I done a lot of work for one of them, and they want to talk to you as soon as you can meet with them.

"Some seismic work will need to be done first to find out how large the oil deposit is. Then based upon that, an exploratory well will be drilled to learn how they'll have to go to reach it. If it's feasible, then a production well can be drilled. Can you meet with them while you're here in Australia?"

Realizing his plans had just been changed; Josh resigned himself to the fact that he wouldn't be going home just yet. "Now is as good a time as any." *I had no idea that the sample would be oil, and now things are moving really fast.*

The three men spent the remainder of the day and into the night going over the details for the geologist and the drilling company president. At the conclusion of the late meeting, it was decided that Frank would arrange to have a seismic team visit the bay. They would establish the reserve area and gather all the measurements.

"All of that will take maybe two weeks and cause some noise problems and most likely, kill a few fish," Frank said.

Josh suddenly realized that all the plans they were making were completely outside the parameters of his agreement with Tam and the islanders. *I'd better come up with a list of things that benefit the people so they'll be in favor of all these changes and disruptions to their lives.*

Chapter 22

After a number of delays, Josh finally departed Australia three days later with a heavy heart. He'd been thinking about what he would tell Tam and his people when he got back. The flight to Bali was three and a half long hours, so he took out his well-used notebook and began to make a list all the things about the oil drilling that bothered him, all of the benefits and all of the things he needed to get done soon. By the time he finished writing, he'd filled four pages and his mind was foggy with exhaustion, so he decided to sleep during the rest of the flight.

Grando was impatiently waiting for Josh when his plane landed at the Bali airport. He was bubbling over with enthusiasm and talking so fast that Josh had to yell at him to slow down. Finally, Grando began to speak in a normal voice and let Josh know that he'd caught three times more fish than he'd ever caught with the old boat. "My new boat makes everything so much easier!"

He then insisted that Josh stay with him so they could celebrate.

Josh had planned to do some much-needed shopping in Bali before going back to the islands, so he suggested Grando accompany him. As they headed out, he called Kyoto to thank Hjosan for his help and friendship and to plan for another visit soon.

After they'd finished shopping and loaded everything onto the boat, they decided to go out to dinner. The two made an early evening of it and retired early since they were early the next morning.

At dawn the next day, Josh slipped the mooring lines of Grando's boat and they slowly headed for the open sea. Josh remained deep in thought during the entire journey. The trip went smoothly and in no time they were docking at Island number one.

Josh remained contemplative the next day, and spent quite a bit of time staring out at the bay. The area where the oil had seeped out, was his focus. The more he stared at it, the angrier he became.

I look out across this beautiful bay, and envision a bunch of oil derricks sticking up everywhere. That's going to disrupt this island paradise and ruin all that I'm trying to do. The islanders certainly won't like it either. They'll probably ask me to leave, and I would totally understand if they did.

"I'll have to wait until the geologist comes and to do the seismic studies. Maybe with the answers that provides I can figure out what to do.

The engineers readying the building site for the chicken and pig shelters brought him out of his trance when they came to ask him when the contractor would arrive. He told them Robert had called him and announced that the final plans were about done and that blueprints were on the way. That satisfied them and Josh went back to staring at the bay.

"Do you know when the materials will arrive?" asked the foreman."

"Those materials and everything for the two apartments were supposed to be shipped as soon as they got everything together. My guess is they're already on the way here."

The construction foreman asked Josh to take a look at the final grading work for the animal shelters. "When we finish here, we'll work on removing the rock littering the floor of the cave. We need to have that done before the shipment gets here. I'd like to get this done for you as quickly as possible, so I can head home for some cold Fosters beer and the warm body of my wife."

When he mentioned the word wife, it made Josh think about Tam's suggestion that he find some island ladies to take care of him. That thought was more than he could deal with right now, so he put it to the back of his mind and headed off to Tam's village.

Somehow, Tam always knew when Josh was coming for a visit. Today, he was waiting at the edge of his village under his favorite coconut tree "Today's a nice day to sit and talk about what's bothering you, Mr. Josh." Tam said amiably.

Josh knew when Tam called him "Mr." Josh it meant he wanted to talk to Josh about something. They took their customary seats under the tallest coconut tree, and one of the ladies brought them some fresh fruit.

As he and Tam made themselves comfortable, there was a loud crash nearby that made Josh jump. A big ripe coconut had fallen from the tree, right next to them. "No worry, dear friend," Tam said, laughing. "When a nut gets so old the stem cannot hold it, down it comes. If you ever get hit by one those, you'll certainly know it."

Josh let Tam start the conversation. "Is all of that noisy work almost done where the animal pens will be?"

"Yes, they're almost finished. They had to move a lot of large rocks to accomplish what we're trying to do. I'm sorry they caused so much noise and took so long to finish.'

"No worries," Tam said casually. "We all just wondered."

Now it was Josh's turn. "I wanted to talk to you about the strange matcrial I found in the bay. I sent a sample to Australia to find out what it was, and they told me it's crude oil."

"What is oil?"

"This type of oil is the base for a lot of fuels, like what makes Grando's boat run. It's something that's extremely valuable to the rest of the world, even if the people here don't really have much of a use for it. While I was in Australia, arranged for a geologist and a seismic crew to come here and take a look at the bay and what's under it to see exactly how much oil is there.

"The main thing that concerns me about this is there will be some loud explosions that will send sound waves down through the water and all the way through the oil deposit. They will then take readings to determine exactly what's down there." Josh used a sand drawing to show how the seismic sound waves were carried to the sea bottom and returned. "They won't do any blasting in the bay. I don't want to disturb the fish or anything else that lives there.

"Until the tests have been completed and the scientists study the information, I don't have much else to tell you. Before I make a decision about what to do if there is a substantial amount of oil under there, I'll sit down with you and the rest of the islanders so I can hear any concerns or suggestions you might have."

"Tam, just want to be sure you and all of your people know why I bought your islands. I wanted to make sure that everyone here is secure and safe for years to come. The potential earnings from this oil would go a long way towards accomplishing that goal."

"Josh, my friend, you always shared your plans with us and have always been honest. I trust that you'll do what is best." He then asked Josh to share the evening meal with the people and Josh gladly accepted. The music and dancing always lifted his spirits and took his mind off his problems for a while.

When the food was served Josh was amazed to see that they'd slaughtered one of the new pigs and roasted it over hot coals. The pork was accompanied by lots of fresh vegetables and fruit. As always, the islands spices made for a meal that no restaurant could ever match.

Chapter 23

The next morning, Tam was at Josh's doorstep first thing. "Dear friend, I couldn't sleep last night. What you told me about the oil was disturbing. I have a lot of questions you need to answer before we can decide what to do. I know you said that nothing would happen until tests were done. The thing is, the drilling that's necessary to perform those tests is what bothers all of us the most. I don't think the people will want drilling to be done unless they know there is enough oil there to make it worth the upheaval it will cause in our lives.

"The people fear that drilling will make the oil come out from under the seabed and then it will ruin our fishing and our beaches."

Josh smiled, relieved that he could ease the islanders' minds. "No, Tam, the drilling won't let the oil come out. It will be a small hole that will probably close back up almost immediately. Tam, I promised you yesterday that I wouldn't let the scientists go anywhere on any of the islands except the cave. Once they've done their tests, they'll tell all of us what the results are. You and all the other island people will be involved every step of the way."

"Okay, we'll just have to trust you, Mr. Josh. I will reserve my worry for after the test results are known."

Tam then looked a bit sheepish and fumbled with his next question. "Have you thought anymore about maybe having some of the island girls come to live with you?"

Josh hesitated for a moment because he hadn't expected this complete subject change. He'd hoped Tam would forget about this, but realized it wasn't going to happen. The best decision that he could now think of was to let Tam know that he had decided to turn the southwest end of the cavern into two apartments, suggesting he would eventually have someone else living there.

Because Josh hesitated, Tam tried again, "Many of the ladies are worried about you living by yourself. There are more than twenty women to each man here, and they just can't figure out how you live that way. They won't leave me alone about this, Mr. Josh. I need your help."

Josh knew that he'd have to do something to meet them halfway or he'd never hear the end of it. He was just too busy to figure it out right now. "Tam, I have so much work to do, and on top of that I need to deal with the scientists when they get here. Can we revisit this subject as soon as the apartments in the cave are completed? Let the ladies know I'm thinking about what I want to do, but won't have an answer for them for a while. Will that keep them off your back?"

Tam just smiled and asked," My friend, are you afraid of the women?"

Josh laughed and said, "No, they don't scare me. I just have so much to do right now that one more thing on the list is just too much. Tell them they'll just have to wait."

The next day, Josh sat staring out at the bay, thinking about his woman problems. An incoming radio message from the soon-to-arrive Australian ship carrying with the building materials shook him out of his stupor. The message was short and simple. "Will arrive your bay early tomorrow. Be ready to offload. Ship needs to return ASAP."

Josh made a dash to the construction foreman's office and let him know about the ship's imminent arrival. The man almost danced a jig. "Finally! Now we can get down to business. All the material is coming, even the stuff for your apartments?" Josh assured him that was correct.

The foreman let him know that a few items had to be moved down at the dock so they'd have a place to offload the massive pile of materials. The foreman got his moving on that, then went to the cave to check that it was ready as well. The materials for the apartments were to be stored inside the cave, so they'd be near where they'd be used. It took just an hour to get everything was in its place. Josh breathed a sigh of relief, knowing they were ready and there would be no delays.

The ship arrived on schedule and the offloading of materials went smoothly. Everything was stacked in neatly and the dock and in the cave, ready for the contractor to begin construction.

The contractor started on the animal pens and shelters first. The cement foundation forms had been set for the pig and chicken shelters, and they were ready to go. It took two days to pour the foundations and set the anchor bolts. Everything was now ready for framing on the two buildings. Within a week, the pig shelter was complete except for the air conditioning.

Josh was always at hand when anything was being done and Tam somehow found time to just sit and watch. As the contractor began the two apartment structures, Tam was surprised by the difference between the animal shelters and Josh's apartments, and he had lots of questions.

"Josh, my friend, how come the walls in your apartment are covered on both sides? And what is that being run from one space to another? How come there are pipes in the ceiling? It all seems rather crazy to me."

Josh knew that Tam was interested in how things were made, so he sat with his friend and explained every detail. Tam still seemed a little confused, "Wait until the apartment is complete," Josh told him. "Once you see the finished product, you will understand it all."

Chapter 24

It took two months to complete basic structure inside the cave, and by that time the things going on outside were posing more questions for Tam.

The material for the septic system had been shipped along with all the other materials. There were many different pieces of piping and the main section was much bigger than Josh had thought it would be.

The real fun began when the flush toilets were installed. The first time, Josh flushed the toilet, Tam jumped back, startled. Then Tam took his turn and got firsthand experience. At first, he hesitated then with a gleam in his eye, pushed the handle down and jumped up and down with pleasure as the water swirled around. The rushing water in the toilet bowl fascinated him, and he had to try it several times. Finally, Josh took his arm to stop him from doing yet again, and began to explain what the toilet was for. It took some time before Tam seemed to understand.

The shower was a whole different story. Tam had never had running water cascading down over his whole body before, let alone water that could be made hot. First he stuck his hand under the running stream and jerked it back as though he'd been bitten. With Josh encouraging him, he stepped under the showerhead, clothes and all. Josh handed him a new bar of soap and motioned for him to use it. Tam didn't understand, so Josh showed him how to apply the soap down his arms and then across his upper body. Once he figured it out, Tam had one of the biggest smiles on his face Josh had ever seen.

A dripping wet Tam finally turned off the water and said, "That was amazing, my friend. How is the water hot?"

Josh explained that pure cold water had been piped from the high lake at the top of the dead volcano. It came down in a four-inch plastic pipe. Josh also told him that he planned to install outlets in the village too. The two-inch pipe had already been run to the edge of the village, but it hadn't been connected to the water yet.

Josh knew he would have to explain the advantage of running water to the to the islanders, which is why he had shown Tam the toilet and shower. If his reaction was any indication, the water would be a big hit.

"The contractors will install the faucets and connect the pipes in the village as soon as they're finished with my apartment. Hot water is in easy to supply; it runs down several of the steam vents and has been heated by the lava. Eventually, if you want it, you will have the same things you've seen in my apartment."

"That's an interesting thought," Tam said, "though I'm not sure everyone will want this. They like the old ways and are frightened of anything new."

"I won't pressure anyone to make these changes. I just want them to know they are available. My goal is to make life better for everyone here."

The evening was coming to a close and as he usually did, Tam invited Josh to share the evening meal and whatever the village people might have in mind for entertainment. Josh had hope Tam would offer, and was quick to accept.

A few weeks later, the foreman doing the work on Josh's apartment told him that he was almost finished. Josh asked him if he had to leave as soon as the job was finished, and he responded, "As far as the boss is concerned, I can have as much time as I think I need. Did you have something else you wanted me to work on?"

Josh told him he'd like to have several shower/bathroom facilities constructed in the village, plumbed with both hot and cold water. "I have all the pipes and we have a lot of cement left over from the animal shelters, so I don't think supplies will be a problem. I just need someone to do the construction. Why don't you come down to the village with me so you can see what I want?"

Josh sought out Tam when they got to the village and the three of them walked around so they could decide the best locations. They eventually planned out three different sites that would make things convenient for everyone.

There was no need to get into details, since these were simple buildings. The only thing they discussed in detail was the size of septic system and how everything would be connected. Josh had already asked the construction boss in Australia to order two more complete systems. He'd been confident he could eventually gain the islanders' approval. He'd been a little surprised by how eager they'd all been to do this.

The additional systems would be delivered with some additional materials for another boat dock. It would be a while before the materials arrived, which gave the foreman plenty of time to get everything built.

Much to Josh's surprise, Tam invited them a special dinner in the village. Tam explained the exception to their stranger rule, saying, "It's to celebrate getting the showers and toilets."

"By the way, what is your name?" Josh asked the foreman. "I'm sorry. I've been so busy, I just hadn't even thought to ask."

"I'm Ralph, just like my father. When I was born, he fought with my mother about naming me after himself. Mom lost."

The grand evening the islanders presented completely overwhelmed Ralph. The wonderful food and the friendly island people amazed him.

Chapter 25

It took a while before Ralph was able to begin construction on the new bathroom facilities. The front loader made digging out the foundations easy work, and they had the cement slab poured along with all the plumbing installed in another week. All that remained was building the outer walls and teaching the villagers how to use the new attraction.

During the construction, most of the villagers stood at a distance to watch the strange goings on. They all seemed to view this activity as grand entertainment.

The final piece of the construction puzzle would be installing the septic system. Thankfully, the shipment was due any day.

A few days later, Josh sat down with Ralph and went over all they had accomplished. When that was done, Josh added several new items to the already long list. "All this, and I haven't even thought about what we'll need if the oil turns out to be viable!"

Josh had come to trust Ralph, so he asked, "Do you know anything about oil and how they bring it up from the ocean floor?"

"Are you thinking about drilling for oil in that beautiful bay? Why do you want to spoil such an untouched area? Do you want to ruin this place?"

Ralph didn't know that he'd already confirmed there was oil under the bay. As they talked about the way drilling is done, Ralph admitted that he didn't know a great deal about how it was done currently, but had done some service work for a drilling company in the past.

"I visited their drilling rig and was amazed by how dangerous the whole operation seemed. The guys that worked on the rigs — roughnecks — certainly earn their nicknames. They make good money and spend as much as two weeks at a time working twelve-hour shifts. That's not for me; I like to come home to a warm bed every night."

Josh and Ralph talked further, and Ralph asked, "Have they done seismic studies?"

"No. What are those?"

"They're a special science and don't always prove anything about what's on the ocean floor. I'm amazed that you're so excited and sure there's oil under the bay when you have done the seismic studies."

That struck Josh as being odd.

"The rig I worked on had two large storage tanks filled with oil that was pumped from the deep well. I don't know how deep it was but they had a large supply of drilling pipe stored on a special steel rack."

Josh was more confused than ever after talking to Ralph. *I need to ask someone about seismic studies ASAP!*

Finally, the new bathroom facilities were finished. Now all they had to do was connect the septic system once the shipment arrived. The shelter for the septic system was also ready to be used as soon as the units arrived. One unit would serve the village system and another might be used for something else Josh had been thinking about. They were cleaning up the construction debris when the ship carrying the septic systems arrived.

Much to Josh's surprise, Paul Mitchell, the engineer, was also on the ship. Mitchell quickly told Josh that he had to see for himself how everything had gone together. He also wanted to sit down with Josh to explain some of the details concerning the oil.

At the mention of oil, Josh felt a chill run down his spine. The whole oil thing had become a subject he almost dreaded thinking about. "Without the seismic proof of oil, who can say what's under the bay? I hope they plan do conduct those before they do anything else."

Ralph helped Josh prepare a giant dinner of fresh-caught lobster and stuffed flounder. Both men had enjoyed this same meal together many times and never got tired of it. The stuffing was made with fresh veg-etables and chopped shrimp. Paul was impressed by the pair's culinary skills, and all three men devoured the feast leaving nothing on their plates.

When they'd finished, Paul asked Josh if he was ready talk some more about the oil.

"What a way to ruin a good meal," Josh responded. "I guess I do need to talk about it so I can finally figure out what needs to be done.

"Ralph and I have talked about what goes on with the drilling process and if he's right, it might cause to much disruption to the islanders' way of life," Josh said, and went on to explain the bargain he'd made with all the islanders."

"It's early to make any decisions," Paula said, "but the scientists and some people from one of the big oil companies want to meet with you and discuss being involved."

"Wait. Since when are the big oil people involved?"

"They smell oil, so they come in for the kill just like sharks," Paul answered. "What exactly bothers you about the process?"

"I'm worried about contamination and that the whole process will change the way the islanders live. They won't allow that, I'm sure."

"I see."

"I also don't see how the drilling can be done without some equipment and people coming onto the island. I don't see Tam or his people going for that, either."

"I'm aware of the obstacles involved," Paul said. "The scientists let the oil guy know that they'll have to deal with you, and only you. Are you ready to get everyone together so we can hopefully make some kind of decision?"

Josh thought for a while, then remembered his friend, Hjosan was well acquainted with a number of Japanese ministers, so he decided that Kyoto would be a good place for the meeting.

"I don't want to meet here, obviously. I have a good friend in Kyoto who can provide the best accommodations and food. I think that's the best place for this meeting. I'll contact Hjosan and then give you the best available dates. You can work with your people and the oil company representative and get back to me. It will take me several days to get this set up. Once I do, I'll let you know the details."

Suddenly many ifs began to cross Josh's mind. *What if there has to be some kind of oil terminal and dock? What if large oil storage tanks have to be built close to the docks? What if they need a pumping station and who knows what else?*

The ever-constant questions running through Josh's mind began to cause him to toss and turn all nigh that night. Finally, he came to the conclusion that if they couldn't prove there was a substantial quantity of oil beneath the bay, then he'd cancel everything. The benefits had to outweigh the negatives.

Early the next morning, he called Hjosan, told him about his predicament and asked for his help. Josh's request piqued Hjosan's interest and he peppered Josh with questions. At last he softly said, "So, it comes down to meeting with these people and figuring out if there's anything to the their supposition."

"That's it exactly. They are supposed to conduct the seismic testing soon. At this point, that's all I know."

"Big questions left unanswered, island boy," he said and laughed.

The talked a little longer and Josh got all the details set for his visit.

Chapter 26

Josh called Grando and arranged for a ride to the Bali airport. As Grando drove, he also had a range of questions that Josh couldn't answer. Josh was beginning to find the whole oil thing extremely frustrating.

The flight to Kyoto was uneventful and only took three hours. Hjosan met Josh at the airport and instantly began with more questions. Josh finally told his friend everything he knew and that he'd learn more details during the planned meeting.

"My friend, the oil business is complicated and the whole world is fighting accumulate as much as possible. Do you have plans for marketing the black gold? I know the energy secretary of Japan will want to have a serious talk with you as soon as he finds out your secret. I can arrange a meeting you when you're ready. This could be an exciting find that might mean a big change for Japan."

Josh made arrangements for rooms to accommodate five or six people at Hjosan's, with an open-ended reservation date. He emphasized the need for complete secrecy.

Hjosan assured Josh that no one would find out anything from him or his people.

Mid-morning the next day, Josh phoned his brother-in-law Robert, who was still on the island, and passed on the details of the arrangements, then asked when the other parties would arrive.

Almost without hesitation Robert asked if he could be included in the meeting too. Josh chuckled and told Robert he'd already assumed he would be there. "I want you to act as another representative for islanders. I'm worried that these big oil people are going to try to railroad me and disregard the islanders all together. I know how these guys operate. I want to be sure they don't pull a fast one, and it would be nice to know that you've got my back."

"You know I do," Robert said. "I'll be there for you and the islanders."

On the flight back to Bali, Josh was still plagued by worries. *I'll be glad when all this is decided. I'm tired of worrying and speculating.*

Grando was waiting to pick him up when his plane landed. As usual, he had lots of questions about Japan and Hjosan. Josh took the opportunity to embellish some of the details, especially the celebrating they'd done the night before.

Finally, he admitted to Grando how worried he was about the oilmen's impending visit. "I need to find some-one who knows about this stuff but doesn't have an agenda or reason to mislead me."

Chapter 27

It was a month before Robert called Josh and asked if May 23-24 would work for the big meeting. Josh immediately assured him that it would and that he would let his friend in Japan know. He also gave Robert the exact address of Hjosan's accommodations. "There's a large room available there that will be great to use for the meeting."

When he finished talking to Robert, Josh called Grando and asked him to send a message to Hjosan with the dates and a request to use the large meeting room. He also and asked Grando to arrange to pick him up on May 21st so he could leave early and get there well ahead of the rest.

Now that everything that Josh had a definite date for getting answers, he began to feel a little better about things. He decided to go and have a talk with Tam and let him know the uncertainty was about to be resolved. Lately, he found himself talking to Tam more and more and they'd become good friends.

Chapter 28

On May 21st, Hjosan met Josh at the airport. They went directly to Hjosan's establishment and he and Josh got things ready for the meeting. Now that the time was near, Josh was feeling calmer and was confident he would get the answers he needed to make the correct decision for all involved.

Josh and Hjosan talked about what would go on and Josh said, "When it comes to dealing with the Japanese Minister of Energy, I want you to be my interpreter and voice. The Japanese culture and language both have many subtle meanings that aren't always obvious to westerners."

"I'd be happy to," Hjosan said.

At exactly eight o'clock on May 23rd, all parties were seated around an oval table in Hjosan's meeting room. It soon became obvious to Josh that the oilmen and scientists had come to some kind of agreement by the way the opening statements were made. This made him wary and he knew he needed to pay strict attention to everything said.

Robert sat next to Josh, with Hjosan seated opposite them. The scientists took charge by saying the preliminary research on the oil deposit incomplete. The seismic test had yet to be done and no one seemed to know whether there was a substantial oil field or not.

This was not what Josh wanted to hear. It seemed like they were trying to get him to agree to something without all the facts. The oil company people just kept talking about what they would do for the islanders. Things like new homes and roads, a ferry to run between the islands, etc. At that point, Josh quit listening and gave both Robert and Hjosan a skeptical look. Both knew that it was Josh's way of saying none of that was going to happen.

Both the scientists and the oil people presented all sorts of paperwork, but what it boiled down to was guesswork. There was a lot of speculation about how much oil might be under the bay, but no real data.

The leader of the oilmen stood up, puffed out his chest and declared, "My company would like to arrange a contract to develop the entire basin and will assume all costs. Of course, we will want to manage and control all the assets. When do you think we might come to some kind of contractual understanding?"

Josh couldn't believe what he was hearing. With as much professionalism as he could muster, he said, "I think we all need to take a break." He then promptly got up and left the room.

Robert got up and followed him, jogging to catch up with Josh who was walking quickly down the hall. "Josh, wait a minute," Robert called out.

When Robert caught up, Josh said heatedly, "I will not deal with these jackasses anymore. My islands are off limits to *all* of them. They have no proof there's actually something substantial under the bay; they just want control of the whole country. I want to put a stop to everything connected to the oil."

By this time, Hjosan had come to stand with them. Josh turned to him and asked if he could set a meeting with the energy secretary and his people as soon as possible.

A smile came over his friend's face. "It will be a pleasure. I can assure you they will listen carefully, unlike those jackals in the meeting room."

"So, what do you want to do about the people waiting for you in there?"

"They can all go straight to hell as far as I'm concerned. I guess, though, I should at least let them know that this meeting is over and that there will be no deal, ever."

Josh didn't bother to sit down when he came back into the room. In his most professional voice, he let everyone know things wouldn't be progressing further. "I made a solemn promise to the people of my country, and no corporation will make me change that. So, gentlemen, my final answer on this matter is a firm no. Thank you for your time." Then he walked out.

That evening dinner, Hjosan treated Josh and Robert to a lovely dinner. They sat for a long time after they'd finished and finally Hjosan asked, "What do you have in mind, dear friend?"

Josh was angry about the whole oil thing. He needed to let off some steam so he could make a rational decision. Finally, tapping the table, he said, "I'm not going to do anything until I meet with the Japanese government people. Depending on what they say, I might hire the Australian drilling company and handle things myself. Robert, the owner's your friend, do you think he'd go for it?"

"We'll have to see, Josh. Get things ironed out and then we'll talk to him."

The next morning Hjosan called the Secretary of Energy in Tokyo, and set up a meeting for Josh. The secretary's assistant answered and told Hjosan there wasn't an available date in the near future. That changed when Hjosan mentioned the outcome of the meeting might mean a serious change in the availability of oil for Japan. Once he heard this, the assistant told him he would call back soon with a date.

The three men were enjoying one of Hjosan's massive luncheons when the waiter called Hjosan to the phone. There was a very short conversation and when

Hjosan returned to the table, he smiled and said, "That was the energy secretary. He asked if tomorrow would be soon enough. He'll meet with you here. He keeps a beautiful young lady in one of my private apartments and hasn't seen her in several weeks. That was probably helped expedite the meeting.

"I'll make arrangements for a special lunch and we can all enjoy a fine time before getting down to business. I am invited, aren't I?"

Josh reached across the table and took Hjosan's hand, "I consider you part of the family. Having you and Robert there with me is important to me. I value your advice and hope you'll help me navigate these difficult waters."

Chapter 29

Just after noon the next day, the Energy Secretary, Mr. Oshimora, arrived for the meeting. Hjosan, Robert and Josh greeted him, and they sat down to a lovely lunch. When they'd finished, they got down to business.

Josh detailed his position and discussed the needs of the people of the Three Islands of Sumwhr. He could see a kind the man was fascinated by what he was saying.

Josh went on to explain that he would always seek the islanders' approval of anything that differed from their traditional way of life. Josh noted that the Secretary was nodding his head as in approval

Mr. Oshimora cleared his throat and softly asked, "Exactly how do you want my country involved?"

"Well, first let me say that at this date we have no concrete proof that there's enough oil there to worry about. If we find there is a substantial field under the bay, then I would like to discuss things further with you. I guess I'm just letting you know there's a possibility that we might have oil to sell to your country."

Josh paused and noted that Mr. Oshimora didn't look as disappointed at this news as he would've expected.

"I know you expected to learn there was a great oil discovery in my new little country, but we haven't made it further than the discovery stage yet. I'd hoped to have more information at this point, but the oil company I was dealing with misled me. I've since let that company know I won't be dealing with them any longer."

Mr. Oshimora smiled and assured Josh that the Japanese way was to take things slowly. "We will wait to hear from you and will keep the needs of your country in mind at all times if we end up working together. I would say we can put the rest of this meeting on hold until you make a decision. There's no harm in that. Now that we're done, I can enjoy my stay with no more thoughts of business."

Josh was pleased and felt the meeting had gone well. The door had been left open for more talks and that was all he could hope for at this point.

Josh and Robert left for the islands then next day. When they there, Josh had a new problem on his mind. "Robert, we need to cancel all material related to the oil situation. I know pipe, generators and various other big pieces of equipment were all scheduled to ship here. I hope cancelling them won't cause you any problems. If anyone asks, just tell them anything related to oil exploration on the islands has come to a dead stop."

"Don't worry about it, I was going to borrow almost all of it from the company's operation in New Guinea, anyway. I'll work everything out with the senior engineer there. They'll probably be glad it's staying. Anything else?"

"I'll pay for any expense incurred because of the cancelation. Just make a list and give it to me and I'll make payment in full."

"That's fine," Robert said and paused. He looked like he had something else to say, but stayed silent.

"What is it, Robert? Whatever it is, I'm responsible and I'll take care of it. No worries."

"No. It's not that. I wanted to talk to you about something else. Ever since I came to your country, I've felt like I belong here. The only reason I haven't said anything about it before is that I wasn't sure what my wife wanted to do. She took care of that problem recently by asking me for a divorce. She got tired of me being gone all the time and decided to make it permanent.

"Is there any chance I could move here and become a citizen of your little country? I realize I'll have to ask Tam's permission, too, but I wanted to talk to you first. This is the closest place to heaven I've ever been, and I just can't stand the thought of having to leave. Will you speak to Tam on my behalf?"

Josh was stunned. This was the last thing he expected to hear. It took him a few emotional moments to find his reply. "Of course. We can talk to him about it right now; he's headed this way."

The two called to Tam and asked him to join them under their favorite tree. They moved over and gave Tam a space between them. After he sat down, the men began their plea. Tam sat with his arms folded across his chest, taking in every word.

When they'd finished, Tam just laughed. "Mr. Robert, for weeks I've been trying to figure out how to invite you to move here. Now that I know you want to, I need to seek the approval from my people. We'll have a meeting soon and put it to a vote, but know that you have my approval now."

Chapter 30

Three days later, the islanders had a meeting to discuss Robert's citizenship. There was a lot of friendly singing and pleasant shouting coming from the village that evening as Josh and Robert listened while sitting under their favorite tree. Then suddenly, as if someone had thrown a switch, all became quiet.

"I wonder if that's good or bad," Robert mused, at bit worried.

Early the next morning, Tam came striding down the path to Josh's home. Robert and Josh had just begun to enjoy a light breakfast as Tam came in and said, "Good morning, dear friends! Do you have a cup of tea for me?"

"Do you have news for me," Robert asked anxiously.

"I'm sure you heard the commotion last night. We were celebrating the approval of your citizenship. I'd like to shake your hand and officially welcome you to the islands."

They shook, then Tam gave Robert hug and pat on the back. "Welcome home!"

After the happy news, Robert went off with Tam to so he could be officially welcomed into the island family.

When they left, Josh sat down on his deck and stared out into space. *This place is so perfect; I don't want it to change. I have enough money to keep things going for myself for a long time, and I'm sure I can provide for any of the islanders' needs a well. I'm tired of worrying about the oil and everything connected to it. I think maybe it would be best for everyone if I just forgot about it. The islanders aren't too thrilled with the idea to start out with and worrying about it is keeping me from enjoying my life.* "It's decided then!" Josh exclaimed, and felt the weight of the world slip from his shoulders.

After his epiphany, Josh got up and hurried to find Tam. He found him walking back up the path to his home, Robert by his side. "Tam, my friend, I think I have good news for you."

"Well, what is it?"

"There isn't going to be any drilling for oil in the bay, ever. I don't want anything to threaten the paradise we have here."

Tam grinned from ear to ear, then shouted, "My prayers have been answered!"

"I think we should pass an official law that says no one can even visit The Three Islands of Sumwhr without our permission. I think that will help protect our way of life."

Tam seemed satisfied with that idea and then insisted that Josh and Robert join the islanders for the evening meal. It would be a celebration of Robert's citizenship. He soon left to make preparations.

Midway through the meal that evening, Tam stood up and announced, "This has been one of the best days in recent memory. Robert will be making this his permanent home, and Josh has informed me that there will be no oil drilling in the bay." The islanders cheered and went back to eating their delicious meal.

As the evening came to a close, Josh and Robert found a comfortable resting spot under their favorite tree. Josh began the conversation by reminding Robert he could choose any of the three islands for the location of his new home.

Robert gazed far out into the bay and bowed his head as to pray, then choked just a little as he said, "Josh, didn't you say that there are 15 to 20 single women per man on the Garden Island? That's an interesting statistic! I may have to find a new woman. How come you haven't found someone to keep you company yet?"

"Well, I've been busy and haven't really thought about it. I think I need to get to know some of these women before I can even think about taking things further.

"Speaking of being busy," Josh continued, completely changing the subject, "I have a list of things I still plan to do for the islanders. I think you should help me with that."

Robert then jumped in and said, "I'd be happy to help. What do you need done?"

"I think the next important thing on my list is building a storm shelter capable of keeping all the islanders safe. Of course, we'll have to get Tam's approval on everything, but I doubt he'll have a problem with this. We still have the front loader you brought, so I thought we'd use it to do some of the heavy work like clearing rocks. The islanders can help, too, by piling the rocks in a central area so the front loader can scoop them up and take them to the bay. Storm season is coming up soon and right now there's only half of the people have a safe place to hole up."

"That's easy enough," Robert responded.

"I'd also like to create a wider, smoother road from the main part of the Garden Island's village to the large garden. Building several carts to transport the vegetables would also be good. Right now, they carry everything in large baskets atop their heads, which means more trips back and forth.

"Those are just a couple of the things I've been considering. You're the only one who knows how to run the front loader, so I think you're guaranteed a job there," Josh joked.

"Those both sound like good plans," Robert said. "Just let me know when you want to start."

It wasn't too long before Tam joined them, as he usually did after the evening meal. Josh began by thanking Tam for welcoming Robert into their family. Then he broached the subject of the storm shelter. "The cave is by far the best place but it has to be cleaned out of all the loose rock and dirt. We have the big front loader that can do most of the heavy work if some of the islanders can pile the small stuff up, that would make things go much faster. I want to make a shelter large enough to hold all of us comfortably and safely.

"I think the space needs enough room for all of us plus enough leftover for food and water storage. There's no way to predict how long we might need to hide out from the storms."

"I think that sounds like a great idea," Tam said enthusiastically. "We are about a month away from the beginning of storm season. The man who chronicles such things has predicted that this is going to be a really bad one. Because of you, Josh, the main base poles of our homes are fastened to a cement slab and are taken down and stored in the cave until the storm has passed, so we no longer have to worry about that. You have correctly seen that the big worry now is the safety of the people."

Josh hadn't yet thought about a safe shelter for all the new boats. That was going to be another top of the list item. *Let's deal with the peoples' safety first and then move on to the boats,* he thought.

Josh, always the planner, asked Robert to brainstorm some ideas for keeping the boats safe. I think the fishermen need to be able to drag their boats out of the bay and store them someplace safe. We have plenty of space, so that shouldn't be a problem. I think we should procure some boat trailers so the boats can just be towed to safety. Do you have any good contacts for that?"

Robert replied quickly. "That won't be a problem, we'll have them shipped on the next supply boat. How many trailers will we need?"

Scratching his graying hair, Josh counted the number of boats, both those of the fishermen, Grando's, and the one they'd given to the neighboring islands' women after the big battle. I think five will do it."

Now Robert piped up and asked, "Do we have to explain all of this to Tam, or can we just do it?"

"I think he's onboard with any plan that keeps the islanders and their possessions safe. Go ahead and do what you need to do."

They walked around until they found a safe place where the boats could be stored. There was a clearing surrounded by tall rocks that would give the boats shelter. "This looks like a good place to put them, Josh said.

"Yep, I think that will work," Robert agreed.

"I think everything will be fine as long as we get things done quickly and prepare for the worst," Josh said. "Hopefully we won't need everything and the storms won't be that bad, but it's better to be safe than sorry."

With their plans solidified, Robert said he'd better go and place the order for the trailers, "I think that the supply boat is due to leave Australia sometime next week. We'd better start making a final list to make sure we have everything we want. I'm going to ask for a couple cases of Foster's beer, so I'll enjoy my storm time!"

Chapter 31

The next day, Tam joined Josh and Robert for breakfast. After they'd eaten, Josh said, "Tam, Robert and I would like you to visit the area where we where we want to put the diesel fuel tank to supply the boats. Remember, we agreed to have ample fuel available for the Indonesian patrol boats, too. We want to keep them happy so they continue to prevent poachers from violating our no fishing zones."

They walked to the area and Tam agreed it would be suitable and not impact anything or anyone negatively.

The week passed all too quickly and they'd made progress clearing the rocks and debris from both the storm shelter cave and the area where they planned to store the boats. The shipment from Australia wasn't due for another week, so all they could do was wait and enjoy life

The day before the shipment was due to arrive, a woman came running to Josh's house, shouting that something was wrong pointing back toward the village. First Josh and Robert worried that something had happened to Tam, but Robert finally understood her panicked cries and said, "She's saying there are strange about to go around the north point of the island."

Josh asked Robert to contact the Indonesian patrol ship and said he was going to get the rocket launcher and a couple of missiles, just in case. "I'll let them know this is sovereign territory with a no fishing zone and they've violated it. The first shot will be a warning…"

It took Josh about ten minutes to get to the point where the boat would pass. He selected a fallen tree leaned across it. As the boat came around the point, Josh took very careful aim and fired just off the boat's bow. He didn't recognize the flag flying from is mainmast, and didn't really care where it'd come from.

When the missile hit the water, there was a lot of activity on the lead boat. Soon, Josh saw they were making a turn and heading away from the island. He packed up his launcher and the remaining missile and headed to the dock so he could talk to the men on the patrol boat when it got there.

The patrol boat apparently saw the retreating boats and sped off to intercept them. Josh watched through binoculars as the Captain of the patrol boarded the lead boat and spoke to its Captain. Heated words were exchanged, but the patrolman made his point and left. Soon after, the fishing boats headed off in the direction they'd come.

The patrol boat headed to the dock, and the captain quickly stepped off as soon as they came along side. Josh told the Captain what happened, and about the warning shot.

The Captain simply said, "I wish I'd been here to see that! That fisherman was pretty ticked off that you'd shot at him. He kept yelling at me to arrest the crazy man with the missiles."

"Josh laughed and said, "I'm just glad they turned around. If they hadn't, I had another missile ready and was going to destroy one of their boats."

"I'm glad it didn't come to that," the patrol Captain said. "I'll report everything to Jakarta and let them deal with it. I'm sure word will get out that a crazy missile man lives here and there won't be many more uninvited visitors!"

Robert and Tam joined Josh as the patrol boat pulled away from the dock. "You did it without destroying anything!" Tam said, congratulating Josh. "That was a much more satisfactory conclusion to the problem."

Chapter 32

The islands were still enjoying good weather as the shipment from Australia came in. The boat trailers, supplies and chickens and pigs were all unloaded and moved to their specific areas. The islanders were excited to have the new livestock and Josh could almost see them imagining the tasty food they'd make.

They also made progress with stocking the storm shelter and gearing up for the coming storm season. When everything was in place, Josh was confident they could stay quite comfortably for several days. It was another worry he could cross off his list, but another larger problem was there to take its place almost immediately.

Apparently, Josh's warning across the bow of the illegal fishermen's boat didn't have the intended results. Rather than warning off all would-be poachers, it set off a storm of threats from neighboring nations. The threats from North Korea, the offending ship's point of origin, came first. It was something to the effect of saying that no tiny upstart country was going to tell the mighty North Koreans what to do.

The first Josh and the islanders learned of this was when the patrol boat captain told them about it and that it had been confirmed. Indonesia's return response was less than friendly as well and indicated that the tiny island nation had support from Vietnam and the United States as well. When word got out, other Asian countries joined in backing The Three Islands of Sumwhr.

Eventually, things got so bad that the matter was headed for the World Court in Hague. Josh found it hard to believe that all these countries wanted to get involved.

After a lot of thought, Josh decided that the World Court was probably the best way to deal with the crazy North Koreans, and went back to his life.

The next thing on Josh's agenda was installing the larger tank for the boats' diesel fuel. He wanted to make it big enough that a tanker could offload directly to it, but make it as unobtrusive as possible so it didn't interfere with the islands' beauty. They also made sure the installation was secure enough to stay put in a storm. When they gave the details to Tam, he was pleased with the plan.

When that was settled, Josh left Tam and Robert to discuss what they were having for dinner and headed to his secret hideaway. There was the finger of land that was covered with old, but graceful coconut trees. One tree in particular made for a great seat, and Josh sat down to watch the sun make its slow descent to the water as the horizon bloomed with color.

As evening slipped into twilight, Josh walked to the widest part of the shore that made up the finger of sand and trees, thought about how he'd come so far in such a short time. Only a few years ago, he'd been in New York City and miserable. He tried to find something he missed about that life, but there wasn't anything. "I am basically happier now than I've ever been in my whole life," he said to himself. It was nearly dark when he began his trek back to his apartment in the cave.

With the most pressing items on his list nearing completion, Josh turned his attention to the women problem on the islands. The women who wanted a man in their lives were extremely dissatisfied and had been complaining to Josh, partly because they wanted him to choose a wife, but also because they wanted a family.

Josh thought about the problem for a long time, the approached Tam with what he was thinking. "There are a lot of young men in Australia who would love to meet the women here. What would you think about letting some of them come here to live?"

"Well, I think we first need to find a woman for Mr. Robert. He is surely lonely," Tam said.

"I can't speak for Robert, but I have no problem with him finding a woman. Let's go find him and see what he thinks."

They walked around the village until they found Robert working on a loose wheel on one of the vegetable carts. The two men told him what they'd been discussing and asked him what he thought.

"I'll give it some serious thought. I've never really considered it until now. I guess I need to get to know some of them."

"I can help you with that, my friend," Tam said and laughed. "I will start sending them to talk to you right away."

The next day, three beautiful young ladies came strolling down the path asking looking for Robert. They'd brought him lunch and stayed to talk. Since they were all beautiful and pleasant to be around, Robert knew he was faced with a difficult decision.

Each day that week, three more beautiful women came to bring Robert lunch. *Tam is making this decision nearly impossible for me,* Robert lamented.

Chapter 33

Grando hadn't visited the islands for several months when Josh heard the full power scream from Grando's engines coming around the point that opened into the bay. Grando was traveling so fast that he almost crashing into dock as he pulled alongside. Grando jumped off his boat and quickly secured it to the dock.

"Grando, what's going on?" Josh asked, realizing something bad was probably coming his way.

At first Grando was so upset he couldn't get the words out. He finally blurted, "All hell is breaking loose in Jakarta! They've got a new president and he's cancelled all previous agreements. He'd also making lots of changes to Indonesia Law. The country is in an uproar. Some of the Indonesian navy slipped out to sea and no one knows where they are. Have you seen their ships?"

Josh was completely numb from the information Grando had just shared. The Three Islands of Sumwhr could have major problems if this new president didn't want to cooperate.

Josh quickly found out Tam and Robert and let them know what was going on. Next, he tried to contact the patrol boat. After many attempts the Captain who had responded when Josh fired on the North Koreans finally responded and urgently requested sanctuary. He said he would explain why when he arrived.

By early afternoon, the patrol boat made its way cautiously to the dock where Tam, Robert and Josh. "I, and my crew, ask for sanctuary in your country," the Captain said as soon as he stepped onto the dock.

"Of course," Josh responded immediately.

Josh surprised when Tam added, "You and your crew are welcome to stay for as long as you need to. We have plenty of food and will find you a place to stay, all that we ask is that you our way of life and obey our laws."

Josh was greatly disturbed by the news and by the reaction of the patrol Captain and his crew. He had world support, but feared it was going to be a giant struggle to protect his country and his people if the new president decided not to honor the former agreement.

"I guess I'm going to have to make a trip to the World Court to re-assert our legal rights," Josh said to his friends. "Grando, can you take me back to Bali so I can get a flight to the Netherlands? I need to get this settled quickly before someone takes advantage of the confusion."

"We'll leave immediately," Grando said.

An hour later, Josh had packed a small bag and jumped aboard Grando's boat. As they headed to Bali at top speed, Grando's phone rang. Before Grando could say hello the caller said, "The new president has declared martial law and no one can leave the country. The airport is closed to all but a few VIPs and anyone who objects is being thrown in jail. Your friend Josh needs to change his plans."

After relaying this news to Josh, Grando called his friend Michael, who had connections at the airport. "Is there any way my friend and I can get on a plane out of Bali?" Grando asked when Michael answered his call.

"There's only one way, and that's on a plane leaving early tomorrow morning. If you can get to my home after dark tonight, I can get you on that flight."

Grando and Josh waited until it was dark, then headed to a dock near Michael's home. They quietly left the boat and headed quickly to Grando's friend's house. When they got there, he explained that a plane filled with VIPs would be leaving in the morning and he would have to sneak them onboard. "We'll pose as baggage handlers, and one of you can stow away in the hold."

"You go ahead, my friend," Grando said. "I wouldn't be much help to you at the World Court and there's no reason to risk being caught just so I can go with you."

Josh reluctantly agreed and then listened to Michael's plan for getting him aboard.

The plan worked well, and no one suspected what was going on. The whole experience was nerve-wracking for Josh, though. He could see the armed soldiers surrounding the plane as they approached. Apparently, though, they weren't paying all that much attention because they didn't notice when three baggage handlers went over to the plane and only two returned.

Josh spent several hours in the cramped baggage hold before the plane finally took off. He knew the flight was non-stop to Spain. He'd leave the plane there and book a flight to Paris. From there he would continue on to the Netherlands. It would be a long haul, but he knew time was of the essence. *I have a terrible feeling that there are people just waiting to take advantage of the islands' lack of protection.*

He'd contacted Reese Vogal before he left. He'd been so helpful when Josh successfully arranged for the sovereign state of the Three Islands of Sumwhr previously and Josh hoped he would help again. He was encouraged when Vogal said he'd meet him at the airport.

Vogal was waiting on the tarmac as Josh left the plane. He greeted Josh and then said, "We're aware of what's going on in Jakarta. I've arranged for you to meet with some of our advisers and some measures have already been put in place.

"This craziness happened so suddenly that there is almost no intelligence available. We really don't know what to expect from this new guy either.

"If it's okay with you, we'll go directly to the meeting. The advisers were notified when your plane landed and should be there when we arrive."

The trip didn't take long, as Josh entered the massive meeting room, he was completely startled to see forty men and some dressed in their traditional robes and finery waiting for him.

Josh gave a brief statement about what he knew and then made a plea for continued sovereign status and protection for his country.

"I am here to make sure that my sovereign status is real and protected by the laws of this court. My country has no military force per se but we do have the ability to protect ourselves. I would just rather we didn't have to. I would you're your backing for keeping unfriendly forces out of our country. Thank all of you gentlemen."

There was a lot of discussion after Josh finished, and Josh just sat down and let them hash things out. Finally, one of the men called Vogal over and had a long, whispered conversation.

When the conversation was finished, Vogal said, "Josh, we need at least two days to gather some intelligence so we know what we're dealing with."

Josh then explained about the Indonesian patrol boat's Captain asking for sanctuary himself and his crew. "We gave it to them, and I'm sure they'll lend support if we need help defending our little country. Also Japan, Australia and New Zealand have looked favorably on our plight. I hope that information helps with your decision."

With nothing left to do but wait, Josh found a place to stay and tried to keep informed about what was going on. After a week, Josh grew impatient and let Vogal know he was going to try to go home. "Just keep me informed and let me know if they ever come to a decision," Josh told him as he prepared to leave.

What he found when he tried to find a way back home was that it was impossible to find any kind of transportation back to the island. The closest he could get was Sulawesi, and island situated between Borneo and the Maluku Islands. This caused him to be in a foul mood.

After a week of his now involuntary stay, Josh decided to take a walk. When he left his hotel, he noticed it there was a lot of noise — people talking loudly and hurrying along the streets. Josh stopped a man as he passed and asked what was gong on. When the man responded, Josh was speechless. Apparently the new president had just been assassinated!

While it was causing a bit of panic for the people of Indonesia, this was good news for Josh and his little country. *Now maybe I can get home,* he thought with more than a little relief.

He turned and headed back to his hotel so make some calls. He hoped to take advantage of the confusion and get a flight out. He was lucky and secured a seat on an early flight leaving the next day. As soon as he'd done that, he contacted Grando and asked him to meet him in Bali so they could head home.

Chapter 34

The next day when Josh left the plane, Grando was waiting for him and was in one of the happiest moods Josh had ever seen. As he got closer, Josh realized why Grando looked so happy — he was more than a little drunk.

Upon seeing Josh, he blurted, "They killed the son-of-a-bitch!"

Grando hugged Josh and praised as if he'd solved the problem all by himself. He assured Grando that he'd had nothing to do with the shooting, then laughed at his drunken friend.

"Let's head to the boat," Josh said. "I think I'll be the one driving, since you've obviously got some more celebrating to do."

Josh was so glad to be home; he felt like dropping and kissing the sand when he stepped off the dock. That feeling of elation was soon replaced by trepidation, since he knew he didn't really have anything to report to Tam and the islanders.

He needn't have worried. The islanders took his news in stride and life went on like usual. Josh went back to dealing with finishing up the things on his list and tried to put the rest out of his mind.

Just when Josh finally felt like he could let his guard down, he heard the ship-to-shore radio crackle and a voice asking to speak to him. "Josh, Vogal here. We've completed part of our investigation and found that the former president received a large sum of money to void your sovereign status so a big company could come in and takeover ownership. They wanted to turn the islands into a vacation spot.

"The court has been made aware of this and has been contacted by a lawyer who says he represents this company. They're still trying to oust you."

"I haven't been contacted about this," Josh said, irritated. "Can you send me a copy of the letter? What am I going to do about this?"

"Actually," Vogal said, "the Court would like to represent you and your country in this matter, if you don't mind. They've dealt with this sort of thing before and should make short work of this matter."

"I think that sounds like a good idea, as long as they keep me informed about what's going on. I don't want to be blindsided by something I don't even know about again."

The two exchanged pleasantries for a bit longer, then ended the call. Josh was furious and frustrated that there was no immediate action available to him. As usual, he went to find Roger and Tam to discuss this latest development.

After explaining what he'd learned, Josh said, "Vogal assured me the World Court people will bring thunder and lightening down on them and this matter will go away. I just hope he's right."

The next day, Grando set out for Bali. He was headed to the only shop that had a fax machine. Vogal had sent a copy of the lawyer's letter and Josh was eager to read it.

When Grando returned from Bali with four copies of the documents, he also had news that a new company had opened an office and now was bragging that they would soon own the three islands and would be making them into a far better vacation resort than Hawaii. "They're also looking for lots of employees and offering high pay," Grando told Josh.

"I was able to grab some of the flyers they were passing out to the local people. I added them to your information and also faxed a copy to Vogal. I hope that was all right."

Josh smiled and said, "It's exactly what I would've done."

Within and hour after Grando's fax, Josh got a call from Tamara or Tee as he liked to be called. He was

Josh's friend in the Indonesian government, and the one who'd originally suggested he buy the islands.

Tee promptly assured Josh that all of Indonesia would the sovereignty of The Three Islands of Sumwhr. "We're ordering two of our newest and most powerful patrol ships to join the one you have there now. That should be enough to ensure your peoples' safety."

Josh was immediately relieved. "Tee, that's the best news I've had in quite a while. Thanks for letting me know."

Chapter 35

Three weeks later, Josh got a call saying a representative from the World Court wanted to schedule a visit. When he asked who it would be, he was surprised to learn it would be Vogal. "Mr. Vogal was impressed with your description of your country," the aid said during the call, "so he wants to see it for himself."

Josh relayed this news to Tam and Robert. They decided all the islanders should greet Vogal. They'd also have a dinner to honor him and show him all the best the country had to offer.

"I think all the islanders should be dressed traditionally," Josh told Tam. "Maybe they can also provide some entertainment to show him your peoples' traditions.

"Robert, you are now considered one of us now," Josh continued, "maybe you can tell him why you wanted to become a citizen. I'll also tell him about some of the improvements we've made and how they haven't affected the way of life or caused any drastic ecological changes.

"I want to be sure that when he leaves, he'll be confident that protecting our country is the right thing to do."

The presentation Josh and the islanders made for Vogal was impressive and he enjoyed himself immensely. Apparently, though, he was even more impressed than they knew because he somehow got the court to move up their case. He called Josh and told him that rather than the year wait he'd expected; the first court date was in just four months.

"Josh, after I toured your beautiful island paradise, I knew I needed to get involved with making sure it stayed just as it is. I wrote a detailed report on my visit and included lots of photographs. I think that helped to expedite things.

"As far as what will go on with the lawsuit, I haven't the slightest idea what their lawyer is planning."

"I'll be there for the whole proceeding. Where will it be held?" Josh asked.

"Indonesia urged the court to consider Jakarta, using the excuse that if it was held in The Hague, it would give the wrong impression," Vogal said, apologetically.

"Well, it is what it is," Josh said dejectedly. "Thanks for letting me know."

They ended the call and Josh sat thinking for a moment. *I should record everything that's happened from*

---

the first time I visited Indonesia to purchasing them the islands and then getting sovereign status. I need to write down everything I can remember. It could be important, and it will definitely establish precedence.

Chapter 36

Time passed, and Josh learned no further information about what was going on. The pressure of the pending legal mess was constantly on his mind, but life went on and he continued with his plans.

One thing that he knew that he had to do was contact Grando to be sure he'd be available when Josh needed to travel to deal with the legal issues. He wanted to be in Jakarta at least three days before any proceedings so he could meet with Tee and all his ducks in a row.

The date for the legal proceedings was finally set, and Josh got there early just as he'd planned. He met with Tee and as told not to worry because and the lawyers had everything under control. "We don't expect any surprises from their side," Tee told him. Finally, Josh settled down. *The world's very best are in full control,* he thought.

That evening, he had dinner with Tee and some of his associates, one of which turned out to be the lead attorney for Indonesia. He told Josh he was personally familiar with his case. "We have more legal documentation for your case than any I've ever worked with. You're in good shape," the attorney said. "I think the company that brought this action is completely out of their minds. Do you have any experience with this type of proceeding?"

"No, and it scares the devil out of me," Josh replied honestly. "Tee has given me some idea, but previously when I did business in the United States, I had advisors who managed all my interests and kept me out of legal trouble."

Soon, the conversation moved on to happier topics and the group enjoyed their meal.

At noon two days later, the Indonesian court opened and attorneys, in full formal dress, robes and caps, were ushered into the courtroom. Tee took Josh by his left arm urged him to relax. "You're strung out so tight I can't even get a good grip on your arm," he joked. "Let's go inside, I've arranged a special seat for you so you can see and hear everything. If anything doesn't seem right, here is a notepad and pen just write it down and I'll take your notes to our attorney when they break. Don't say anything to anyone, especially to the lawyer for the opposition. They'll try to get you to make any kind of statement and that could damage our case. Any questions?"

"No, I think I'm ready for this," Josh said, sounding anything but ready.

Josh's seat was on the isle, in the third row. *This looks more like a circus than a court proceeding,* Josh thought. Five of Indonesia's most important lawyers sat in the front row along with two of the World Court's attorneys. The supreme legal authorities were off to the left side. Sitting stiffly on the other side were the lawyers from the company that had brought suit against Josh's country.

One of the Indonesian lawyers stood up, pounded a wooden hammer on the podium and in a loud, strong voice announced, "The court will now come to order."

Everyone in the room was immediately quiet. The all of the legal eagle-types had satchel-like cases in front of them, and they all reached out to open them. Josh thought things would get started as each law group began to shuffle through their stack of papers.

This went on for several minutes, then one of the Indonesian lawyers, a giant of a man, stood up, pounded the gavel again and said, "The purpose of this court is to render a firm legal opinion in the matter before us, with the world court being the final judge." He then added, "This lawsuit was ordered by a Euro Conglomerate, with the purpose of legally overturning the sovereignty of the Three Islands of Sumwhr."

Next, Mr. Vogal explained the location of the islands and that Josh had legal ownership of the islanders and had petitioned for and received status as a country. "As you have noticed, the World Court is represented here, and will participate in the proceedings. This is a serious issue and Indonesia is committed to making sure this matter is addressed and settled completely.

The next item up was the reading of what Euro Conglomerate hoped to achieve and why. This continued into the afternoon. Finally, Josh had heard enough legalese and needed a break. He signaled Tee, then said he needed to take a walk and try to clear his head. "Do you think it would be okay if I miss all this blabbering?"

"It should be fine. All of this is in the paperwork, so there won't be any surprises at this point."

Josh decided to walk around Jakarta for a little while. He was surprised by the poor living conditions of the area where he talked. It nearly made him physically ill witnessing the abject poverty. He continued to wander, wondering why things were so bad here.

Josh suddenly realized he'd been away from the court for several hours and quickly headed back. *I'm such an idiot! I hope I didn't miss anything important,* Josh scolded himself.

As he re-entered the courtroom, it was like he'd never left. The lawyers were still droning on and on. Vogal came to meet him, and asked, "Did you have an interesting walk? I hope you feel better. You didn't miss anything. The lawyers seem to be having a contest to see who can use the most words to completely avoid talking about the real issue at hand! I'm just about ready to stop them, this has gone on long enough.

"The attorney for The Hague wants to countersue for $10 million. That's probably what's next up on the docket. I'm sure that will result in even more blabbing from Euro Conglomerate's lawyers."

"In that case," Josh said, "if I'm not needed, I would like to go back to my hotel. I've had enough of this for today."

Vogal understood and admitted that most court cases were fiascoes just like this. "I've become immune to the stupidity. There isn't anything we can do about it; this is just how court here is conducted. I'm sorry, I know this is stressful for you."

Josh said his goodbyes and left for this hotel room. *I don't think I even need to be here,* he thought. *It would be better for my mental health to just let the lawyers do their thing.* That decision made, Josh located Grando told him he was ready to head back to the islands.

Chapter 37

It took three months of courtroom haggling before the Indonesian officials had also had enough. Finally, the Hague Court stepped in and formally issued their countersuit. Shortly after that, Euro Conglomerate realized it would cost them millions either way, and decided to drop their lawsuit. It was finally over, and Josh's sovereign state was now recognized around the world.

Josh received a copy of the formal report in a gold bounded folder and a note from Vogal, asking if he could pay a visit to the islands soon.

One good thing to result from all the legal wrangling was the Indonesian government assigning two of its newest and best patrol ships to Sulawesi for patrol in it's sovereign territories, which included The Three Islands of Sumwhr. These ships would challenge any unauthorized ships in those waters.

When Josh told Tam and Robert Josh about the new patrols Tam said, "We need to show our appreciation for all this extra security. We should invite the crews of these ships for a big island-style dinner in their honor."

Josh agreed with this plan and notified the ships' crews as quickly as possible.

A week later, the festivities were planned and the patrol ships were expected shortly. The crews were appreciative of the dinner and ate their fill of the island cuisine while being entertained by traditional dances.

Chapter 38

For three months, all was calm. The patrol boats had a regular schedule, and stopped at the island often to refuel and get supplies from the islanders.

At the start of the fourth month, Josh got an urgent message from one of the patrol boats, "Several unidentified fishing boats have been sited few miles from your no fishing boundary. So far, they've given no indication they plan to turn around."

Robert and Josh checked their charts to figure out where the boats were headed and decided to be ready for the intruders. If the patrol boats couldn't discourage these intruders, then Josh would fire a missile across their bow to get the point across.

Early the following morning, the patrol boat reported that one of the boats had fired on them and they'd returned fire, sinking two of the boats. The final word from the patrol boat was, "All is well. The other boats have turned around. There was no identification on any of the boats."

Josh and Tam decided to reward the patrol for protecting them and planned another dinner. For the next two days, the people worked to prepare the best celebration ever made. The patrolmen were appreciative of the dinner and vowed to continue to protect the islands the best they could.

By mid-February, the work on the storm shelter was finally done — just in time for the storm season to start in March. "When there are really big storms on the way, we usually receive three or four day's warning," Tam told Josh and Robert. "The big storms come from the northeast, so we know what to watch for."

The first two storms of the season were mean enough to make everyone on the islands disassemble their houses and store them in the shelter. All of their plans worked well, and both the people and boats were kept safe from the weather. The islanders turned these times into storm-induced sleepovers that usually turned out to be big parties. Even the animal shelters came through the storms well.

The biggest storm hit and left them in the shelter for three days. This storm caused some damage to the cave where they sheltered. Some of the rock from the roof came down, but the front loader made cleanup relatively easy. Within a week, everything was back to normal.

Chapter 39

A few weeks later, Josh and Robert had noticed that there was a lot of activity in Tam's village. The two decided to investigate. Six women from the village blocked their path before they got there. The women explained that Tam was ill and no one knew what was wrong with him.

"We might be able to help him," Josh said, trying to go around the women.

"This is island business," one of them said. "You need to stay away."

Josh muttered to Robert, "We've never experienced this kind of rejection before. Something must be terribly wrong."

No matter how much the two argued with the women, they were still denied access to Tam. Finally, Josh and Robert headed back to the house and sat on the bayside patio all day worrying about their friend.

Near dusk, two older ladies from the village approached. The eldest said, "Our friend wants to make sure a new leader will take his place. We've decided the new leader should be a woman from the Garden Island. That is why we insist that only people from that island address him in his final hours."

"Is Tam really dying?" Josh asked.

"Not exactly. He has learned much from you knows how important it is to plan ahead. He is getting older and wants to be sure everything is in place before his time comes. Tam is concerned about making sure that our history is properly recorded." When they'd finished delivering this message, the women turned and left.

Josh and Robert were thunderstruck. They retreated back to the patio. "What do you think about this? Josh asked Robert.

"If could mean total chaos and undo everything Tam has allowed us to do for the people. On the other hand, it could be a smooth transition. We have no choice but to wait and see."

Tam sent word to Josh and Robert asking them to visit him the following day. "

When Josh and Robert got to Tam's house, he was sitting up and looking fit. "Dear friends, my body is telling me that it my time here is limited. I have no choice but to select the best person to be my successor. This way I can teach them everything I know. Don't worry, I'll be sure to tell the new me exactly how much you've done for our people.

"I came to the conclusion that I must select a woman; they're in the majority so they should decide things. This decision is turning out to be trying and difficult. I would appreciate your thoughts on the matter."

The three men sat down and compiled a list of attributes they thought Tam's successor should possess. Once that was done, they made a list of island women who possessed the characteristics they'd listed. As Tam had said, it would be a difficult decision.

After they had all the names, the three men discussed the pros and cons of each woman's qualifications. When they'd finished with this after several hours of discussion, Tam quietly selected the one woman he felt best met all of the qualifications necessary to be a good leader for his people.

He knew his selection wouldn't please everyone, but wasn't prepared for the opposition from 40 ladies on the Garden Island. This group flat out refused to acknowledge Tam's choice and said they would not acknowledge her as their leader.

Josh and Robert cautioned that this opposition would make things difficult. Tam sadly agreed.

A week later, Tam allowed every soul on all three islands to believe he'd died. In reality, he was still quite alive, but wanted to allow his successor a chance to take-over while still lived and could help with any problems that came up. It seemed that everyone on all three islands was holding their collective breath, waiting for the chaos to begin.

For three weeks, things ran smoothly, if not exactly quietly. There was a lot of shouting and arguing amongst the islanders, but no violence. No one visited Josh and Robert during this time or asked them what their opinion was. Both Josh and Robert had decided it was best to let the new leader come to them, so they stayed out of the fray.

Chapter 40

Two months had passed since Tam made everything think he'd died. The islanders were now aware he was still among the living and politically things had settled. So far, things were going along much as they always had, with the people on islands one and two ignoring the squabbles between the leader and the women on the Garden Island.

When the latest supply ship arrived carrying more chickens and pigs, both men and women pitched in to move them to their respective shelters. Everyone cooperated and got things done, but did notice there was no help from the Garden Island.

Just when Josh and Robert had decided everything would be all right with the new leader, she and five women came to Tam's village. They let it be forcefully known that many things were soon going to be different.

Josh and Robert ignored the five women and headed to Tam's home, where Tam was sitting on his favorite bench. As they approached, the one of the women stepped in front of them and said, "That's as far as you go."

"We're just here to speak to our friend, Tam," Robert told them calmly.

Tam rose and in softly, "Sorry, dear friend, the women of the Garden Island voted and Dana is now their new leader."

"I see," said Josh. Turning to Robert, he said, "Let's go."

Weeks passed and Josh and Robert weren't allowed to speak further with Tam. They stuck to the area around Josh's house and the apartment in the cave, and kept to themselves. No one from the new leader's group approached them.

One day, a horn melancholy sounding horn rang out. "I wonder what that means," Josh said as he and Robert sat on the patio at his house. "I think we'd better go find out what's going on."

They headed off toward Tam's village at a quick pace. They were sure the horn meant something bad. Their suspicions were confirmed when several women met them on the path and told them Tam had passed on to the other side.

Josh expressed his sympathy at Tam's passing, as did Robert. "Is there something we can do?" Josh asked, "We'd be happy to help with his funeral."

"This is island business, you aren't welcome," one of the women stated flatly, then the group turned around and headed back to the village.

"Well, I guess it's pretty clear we aren't wanted here," Josh said sadly. "I'm not sure what this will mean, both for us continuing to live here and for further improvements to the islanders' lives."

When they got back to his home, Josh contacted Grando and let him know what had happened. He also asked Grando to pick them up for a trip to Bali the next day.

The following morning, Grando's boat guided up to the dock and Robert and Josh quickly stepped over the railings and onto the deck. Josh shouted, "Let's get out of here, Grando!" as they quickly stowed their luggage.

Grando looked at Josh questioningly, but simply said, "Bali here we come." He could tell Josh wasn't in the mood for questions, so he kept quiet for the time being.

They were almost in Bali before anyone said anything. Finally, Josh said, "The first thing we need to do when we get there is lease an apartment." Grando just frowned in response to this statement.

After they docked in Bali, Josh and Robert were able to find a nice apartment near the dock, which also meant that it had easy access to the local airport. With that settled, Josh phoned Tee in Jakarta to let him know about Tam's passing and what was happening on the islands.

The first and important item on Josh's list was phoning Mr. "T" in Jakarta to let him know what had happened and was going on with the mess on the three Islands. Once he heard the news, Tee asked Josh to meet with him as soon as possible.

Josh and Robert discussed the potential future for them on the islands for quite some time. "What will you do if it turns out we can't continue living there?" Josh asked. "Will you go back to Australia?"

"Hell no! There's nothing for me there now. I've found a more pleasant way to go through time and don't want to move backwards. If we have to, we can find another place to live here until this is straightened out. I'm sure the government will do everything they can to continue with you in control."

The next day, Josh and Robert met with Tee in Jakarta. "What went wrong?" he asked, as they got straight to discussing the issue at hand.

"Tam tried to make sure things would go smoothly by selecting a like-minded successor, but he was out voted," Josh explained. "A woman named Dana is now in charge, and she's not too friendly to outsiders. We weren't even allowed to attend Tam's funeral."

"What will you do with the ownership of the islands if they continue to exclude you?"

"I'm not sure. Robert and I have been talking about it and we think Dana forced her way into the leadership roll. We don't think the majority of the islanders really want things to be handled this way. I can't really do anything about it, though. I bought the land, but not the people who live there."

"That's true, but you've done so much for them. It's odd they would suddenly decide they don't want you there."

"I'm going to wait a couple of months and see what happens. By then, the women should've had enough time to figure out how to run things smoothly. If not, maybe the people will remove her from the position. If things stay the same, then I'll move to Bali and let the government deal with them.

"If it comes to it, I'm willing to transfer my ownership to Indonesia with no strings attached, though the thought of doing that makes me sick to my stomach."

Chapter 41

Josh and Robert waited for two months to return to the islands. They both missed the paradise and the homes they'd made there. When the time came, Josh asked the patrol boat Captain to visit the island and see what the mood was there. The Captain reported the new ruler and her enforcers did not greet him warmly.

After receiving that report, Josh sadly told Tee he was ready to turn things over to the Indonesian courts. Unlike Josh's previous experience with this country's court system, the proceedings for dealing with The Three Islands of Sumwhr's new leadership moved quickly. The decision was made to send troops to deal with the new island leadership.

Josh let Tee know the troops could use the accommodations in the cavern. "The storm shelter should be big enough to hold them all. I hope you'll make sure the islanders who aren't involved with this new leader will be safe from harm."

Tee assured Josh that he would personally make sure the islanders weren't then you can return to your lovely home."

Two weeks passed and Josh had heard nothing about how things were going. Josh had taken a walk and was thinking about contacting Tee when he noticed the patrol boat coasting into the harbor. Tee stepped off as soon as it pulled up to the dock, and the Captain followed, handing him some papers and a camera.

Tee came over and greeted Josh and asked him if there was someplace he they could to talk. They passed by Josh's apartment and asked Robert to join them, before heading to a small coffee shop.

"I haven't read the papers the Captain just gave me. I wanted you to read them first, then we can discuss what we learn. Before we do that, though, I want you to know that I haven't had any official contact regarding the island situation.

"I do know the military was given orders to do whatever was necessary to settle things in Indonesia's favor. I also know things have gotten worse on the island. Dana has issued an order that no man is to set foot on Islands one and three. She's also been restrained by force on more than one occasion since the military got there. Now, let's go through these papers and see what else we can learn."

As they slowly read the first page, Josh's face turned white. The Captain had been forced to restrain several of the women.

Tee turned to page two and his frown deepened. "Josh, the Captain clearly states that he and his men had nothing to do with what happened next."

The Captain's notes clearly stated that Dana and seven of her cohorts had declared war on the opposing women and all of the island's men. Apparently Dana said she was going to rewrite islands' history, which caused many of the women to stand up to her and disagree — and the battle was on. The Captain reported that 320 of the islanders were not in favor of Dana's leadership.

At this point, apparently, Tam's chosen leader, Masilla, stepped forward and challenged Dana. Her contention was that Tam selected her and she was the legal leader.

The Captain's account continued, saying Dana struck Masilla with some sort of gardening tool and killer her. This was the first and only murder to ever be recorded in the islands' history. After seeing this, several ladies took up gardening tools and began striking Dana, eventually killing her as well. Once Dana was dead, her followers were quick to surrender, claiming they were bullied into following Dana's lead.

The shocked men read on. After the frenzy died down, one woman spoke up and said they needed to find a new leader who embodied Tam's leadership style. The Captain's note said that almost in unison, the people began to shout that they wanted Josh and Robert to return and guide everyone just as they had done before Dana forced them to stop.

The Captain concluded his notes with the information that the islanders wanted Josh and Robert to help them decide what qualities to look for in a new leader and then help them to choose that leader. They will settle us down and work with whomever we choose as our leader.

"Well, I think those islanders are pretty smart," Tee said. "I think the two of you should return and do what they've asked. The government has always been in favor of what you've been doing with the islands, and apparently the people there have been too.

"I think you should inform the government about what happened and withdraw your suggestion that the government deal with the islands. I'll help you with that."

Tee made good on his offer to help. The members of the government seemed relieved that things had been resolved. When the final decision was made and written into the law books, Josh was again in control of things and the government had given him authority in writing.

When the proceedings were finished, Josh and Robert met Grando at the dock, where he'd loaded most of the supplies they'd accumulated while waiting to return to the islands.

Somehow word of their return had beat them to the island. As Grando's boat, approached the harbor of Tea

Island they saw all the smiling faces of the islanders waiting for them on the beach. Josh smiled too, thinking about returning to his home in paradise and all the great people who lived in his country.

A petite woman stood on the edge of the dock waiting to welcome them as they left the boat. She cautiously stepped forward and shook Josh's hand. "Welcome back, Josh. My name is Wanda, and I have been selected to help you get things back on track here. We're all depending on you and Mr. Robert to guide us to a bright future.

"We've already selected a group of potential leaders for you to choose from. They're waiting for us at Tam's house. Please follow me."

Both hesitated, but then Robert nudged Josh and they began to walk with Wanda. When they entered the home, Wanda said, "I think these gentlemen have agreed to help us, so you all need to introduce yourselves."

When the introductions were made, Josh said, "We won't you how to lead your people, but we will give advice about what we feel is best when we're asked. Of course, we'll also always be ready to help you with anything you need.

"I think we need to have several discussions to get a feel for what you hope your leader will accomplish and how things should be done. Maybe we should have the first meeting right here, first thing tomorrow."

Early the next morning Wanda and three other women, one from each Island, were at Tam's old house ready to meet. Wanda explained her companions to Josh and Robert by saying, "Last night when most of the ladies and I were discussing our future, we decided that one representative from each Island should participate in these meetings and have a say in how our future is going to be managed. I hope that you don't mind that we did this without you."

Josh found it strange that he was more or less holding court with four very pleasant women. "First, we need to decide what the most important issue will be. Each of you needs to contribute to this discussion."

As each woman voiced her opinion, Josh listened carefully and concluded that their concerns were in line with Tam's way of doing things. He was relieved to see this and had hope that things would work out.

The end of the long day with a lot accomplished, Josh felt that he should say something in closing. "I hope you know that Robert and I will do our very best to help unite the islands' people and move things forward in a positive way."

"We're happy to hear that," Wanda said. "We couldn't ask for anything more."

www.ingramcontent.com/pod-product-compliance
Lightning Source LLC
Chambersburg PA
CBHW070505120726
47910CB00003B/1126

9 781604 149258